PRAISE FOR DARRELL PITT

'I found myself laughing out loud which rarely happens.'
Sondra Kerby

'An amazing book that has all the elements
of a great whodunnit.'
Ursula Sorensen

'I'm very much looking forward to reading the next book in
the series.'
Alice Hazelbaker

'This was a fun book to read. It had me laughing
a lot throughout.'
Sandy Mill

' I look forward to future installments.'
Caley Gredig

'What an awesome book!'
Michelle

BY DARRELL PITT

The Boy from Earth
Balloon Girls
A Toaster on Mars

Teen Superheroes
Book I: Diary of a Teenage Superhero
Book II: The Doomsday Device
Book III: The Battle for Earth
Book IV: The Twisted Future
Book V: Terminal Fear
Book VI: The Invisible Weapon
Book VII: The Alpha Project

Teen Superhero Bounty Hunters
Book I: Snakebite
Book II: Fear Fight
Book III: Stormfront
Book IV: Past Shadows
Book V: One Small Step

DARRELL PITT

Rings, Rocks and Murder

A ROSIE RYAN COZY MYSTERY

BOOK TWO

KENT STREET PRESS

kentstreetpress.com

This edition published by Kent Street Press, 2025

ISBN: 978-1-923360-40-2 (paperback)

ISBN: 978-1-923360-31-0 (ebook)

A catalogue record of this book is available from the National Library of Australia.

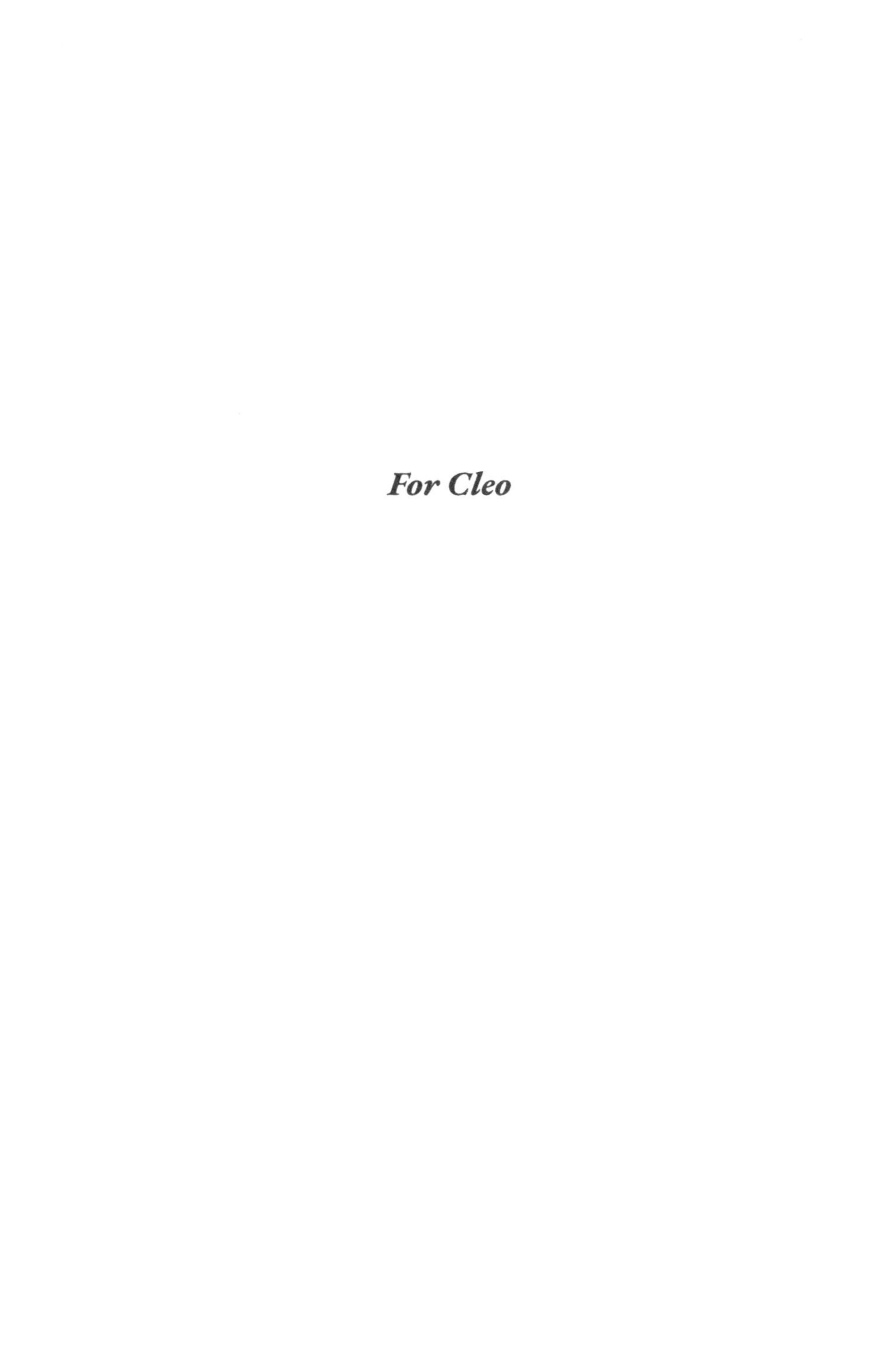

For Cleo

1

'I am now officially the happiest woman on Earth,' I said.

I was sitting in front of Sandy's Diner. Despite it being late autumn, the sky was clear and blue. The kind of day that made me glad I was alive. Sitting opposite me was my best friend Kim Chen, but neither she nor the weather was the reason for my happiness.

Sandy Clementine, the owner, came over with my coffee and a water bowl for my dog, Trixie. My beagle eagerly lapped the water as I took the first gulp of my jumbo double-shot caramel latte.

'Rosie Ryan,' Sandy said. 'That's a very odd grin on your face.' She eyed Kim. 'Has she just been to a champagne break-fast or...'

'Alcohol is not involved,' Kim assured her.

'Who needs alcohol when I've got one of these?' I asked, taking my newest acquisition from a box.

One of these was my new handbag, a *Russell Fletcher* winter edition made of high-quality black faux leather. Not only did it have thirty-four compartments, but also a lifetime guarantee. The bag had been delivered by courier this morning. I patted my chest. 'Be still, my beating heart.'

'How much did it cost?' Sandy asked.

'Er,' I said evasively. 'A bit.'

'Rosie's credit card went Chernobyl,' Kim said flatly. 'A *total* meltdown.'

'Quality costs,' I pointed out. 'And good quality costs a lot.'

Sandy peered more closely at the object of my undying love. 'That's a lot of pockets,' she said. 'Don't you think it makes it easier to lose things?'

I didn't want to admit that handbags with lots of pockets were a personal fetish. 'A girl can never have too many pockets.' I showed them my old bag. 'This old lady has served me many years. Despite having only twelve pockets, my old *Clarissa Taylor* was my pride and joy. But all things must end, and every ending is a new beginning.' I transferred items to my new bag. 'There's my purse...tissues...keys...phone... ah, there's that lucky charm...I wondered where that went...oh, and a packet of...oh, haven't needed them for a while....'

Sandy's only response was *hmm* as she disappeared back into the diner.

'Rosie,' Kim said. 'I love your bag, but we need to talk.'

I glanced up. 'About what?'

'Chris Dawson.'

'Huh?'

Kim leaned close. 'You remember,' she said in a low voice. 'He's co-authoring the book with Katy Dark. I told you about him.'

Both those names rang bells, but one peeled with far more volume. There weren't many people who didn't know the famous Katy Dark. In addition to starring in three Australian films, and surviving a season of Australia's Survival Island, she had just signed a big deal to appear in a new Hollywood blockbuster.

This week, while Katy was vacationing at Cape Carson's Lighthouse Inn, I was joining her entourage to do a series of stories that my editor, Harry Blackshore, was calling, *A Week with Katy Dark*. During that time, I'd conduct interviews with her and the people around her. Among that group was the lesser-known Chris Dawson, who was co-authoring her biography.

'Oh,' I said, the lightbulb finally going off in my head. 'I remember.'

'How could you forget?' Kim asked. 'I met Chris when I was sixteen and he was eighteen. He was visiting Cape Carson with his parents. I was swimming at Shelly Beach when I got a cramp, and Chris helped me to shore.' She sighed. 'It was love at first sight. We spent that whole summer together. When it ended, we made a lot of promises, but we were both young. His parents took him back to Sydney, and I never saw him again.'

'And now he's returning to Cape Carson,' I said. 'Kim, what are you expecting to happen?'

She pushed back her black hair. 'I don't know,' she said. 'Maybe nothing. Maybe something. But I've got to move on from Robert. He's getting married to Alex. They're going from strength to strength.' Her bottom lip quivered. 'And what am I? An old maid working at the library—'

'Kim. You're not an old maid. You're the same age as me: forty-three. And being a librarian is an important job. You're the last arbiter of truth in a world where some people believe the Earth is flat.'

'I know I'm being silly. It's just...' She shook her head. 'Have you ever wondered how your life could have been different?'

I thought about my own marriage. It had fallen apart too. After twenty years, I'd caught my husband George having an affair with Blossom, his secretary.

Yes, my life could have been different, but then I wouldn't have had my daughter Amanda, and I wouldn't have finally ended up living here in Cape Carson. But life for me was good—perfect was too much to expect—but it was good.

Kim continued. 'Rosie, what if Chris had returned to Cape Carson all those years ago?' she asked. 'What if we'd gotten married? Had kids? My whole life would have been different.'

'You've got two wonderful kids.' They lived in Melbourne and were doing fine. 'You can't regret anything.'

'I don't,' she said, peering across at the horizon. The ocean was clear and flat today. 'But a girl can wonder. Anyway, I've got to meet him while he's here.'

'Okay,' I said.

'But I haven't contacted him.'

'Why?'

'What if he doesn't remember me? I'd be mortified. What if that summer has flown from his head completely?' She shook her head. 'No. I need to accidentally bump into Chris. Then...who knows? It could be love at first sight—again.' Kim's eyes fixed on something. 'And talking about love....'

I followed her gaze. Todd Parker, the very handsome sergeant at Cape Carson Police Station, was on the other side of the road. He saw us looking, smiled, and gave a small wave. Built like the Hulk, his police uniform only *just* contained his bulging physique.

I looked a little closer. Maybe I was imagining things, but Todd looked *slightly* less musclebound than when we'd first met. Perhaps he'd been spending less time with the weights and more time enjoying coastal living.

'Kim,' I muttered. Nothing had happened between Todd and me. I think it was partly because Todd was a cop, and I worked for the paper. He probably saw a relationship with me as sleeping with the enemy. We'd also butted heads on more than one occasion; I suspected we were too much alike. 'Todd and I are just friends.'

'Sure you are,' she said, nudging me.

'You're an idiot.'

'But a *smart* idiot,' Kim said, laughing. Todd crossed the road, and Kim took this as her signal to make a getaway. She said a quick *hello-goodbye* before racing off.

'Hey,' Todd said.

'Hey you,' I replied.

Trixie barked, and Todd gave her a pat, his eyes crossing to my two handbags. 'Been stealing handbags again?' he said. 'You know that's illegal?'

'Really? I had no idea.'

'Mind if I join you for coffee?'

'Go right ahead.'

Todd sat and ordered. Contrary to my own caramel lattes, Todd always drank espressos. I don't know how he did it. Just the thought of short black coffees made my face implode.

His drink arrived, and I watched him take a sip.

Amazing, I thought. *No implosion.*

'So,' I said. 'Are you ready?'

'Ready?'

'Todd.' I levelled my gaze at him. 'The Cupcake Festival. You know it's this week?'

'Uh, yes.'

'Well?'

He stared at me in utter confusion. 'Okay. What have I missed?'

I sighed. 'The Annual Cape Carson Cupcake Festival brings visitors from all over the Victorian south-west,' I said. 'It's one of the biggest events of the year. It also results in more threats, bad blood, jealousy, and acts of outright violence than any other event.'

'The Cupcake Festival?' Todd said the words as if trying to wrap his lips around a foreign language. 'This is the thing where everyone makes cupcakes, there's a contest, a parade and—'

'And murders.'

'What?'

'There's been no less than two murders over the years. One was decades ago when old Mrs Jacobs laced a pink frosted buttercream cupcake with enough strychnine to kill an elephant. Her victim was her next-door neighbour, Mrs Perkins. She claimed that Mrs Perkins had stolen her recipe, although that was never proven.

'The second murder was only six years ago when poison was also used, but it was less obvious. Mrs Lansing discovered her husband Carl was having an affair with his business partner. She put weed killer into Carl's cupcake, hoping the police would think it an accident. As it turned out, they didn't.'

Todd was staring at me as if waiting for a punchline. 'Hang on, Kim,' he said. 'You're not kidding. Two people have been murdered over...cupcakes.'

'The most recent one was solved by Wanda Gibson, who used to run the library.'

'Okay,' he said. 'Some people may be as nutty as fruit-cakes—'

'Or cupcakes, as the case may be.'

'—but I'm sure that between the other officers and myself, we can handle—'

My phone beeped. 'Oh,' I said. 'I've got to get to work. And, yes, I know. It's embarrassing to call in reinforcements.'

'Reinforcements?'

'Let's not forget the riot of seventy-seven.'

'The—*what?*'

'The riot of seventy-seven.' After gulping down my coffee, I stood and flung my new handbag over my shoulder. 'Cupcakes are serious business here in Cape Carson. The festival brings out the best and worst in people. Be prepared for anything.'

And upon saying this, I headed off to work.

2

'I'm here!' I announced loudly as I marched through the front door of the Cape Carson Gazette. Trixie gave an excited bark. 'And Trixie too!'

Doris Glow, the paper's seventy-year-old receptionist, glanced up from her desk. 'So I see,' she said. 'Rosie, the phone has been ringing off the hook, and you've already got a few messages. But I know Harry wants to speak to you.'

Harry Blackshore, the paper's editor, yelled from his office. 'Has my favourite reporter arrived?' he asked. 'Send her in.'

Favourite reporter?

This could only mean one thing—trouble. I leaned into Harry's office. 'You called?'

'Grab a seat.'

Harry waved me into a high-backed chair that was jammed between stacks of back issues of the Cape Carson Gazette. *If he doesn't clean up this place soon, he'll end up buried under one of these stacks.* Trixie laid her head on my knee, and I ruffled her neck. Harry's office wasn't her favourite place. Not enough room and too stuffy.

'How's it going with Katy Dark?' he asked.

My heart sank. The last person I felt like talking about was Katy Dark. 'Well,' I said. 'I haven't spoken to Katy yet. Only her publicist, Cindy Hillspring. It looks like she's bringing quite an entourage with her, including her husband.'

'Cameron Dark? From that TV soap opera?'

'Horseshoe Farm,' I said. The program ran for twelve years. Cameron Dark, the lead actor on the show, had been written out after getting married to Katy. 'I never saw it. Soaps aren't my thing.'

'At least you know Katy,' Harry said.

'Oh, yes,' I said absently. 'I know Katy.'

'And not only will we have a movie star, but Spud Butler's arriving in a few days too.'

Spud Butler was an Australian country singer who was coming to Cape Carson as part of the Cupcake Festival. The festival's highlight would be his live performance on Percy Street of his song Mabel's Cupcake Shuffle. The town was trying to set a world record for the most people dancing to the song.

'Yep,' I said. 'Great.'

Harry's eyes fixed on me. 'Okay,' he said. 'What is it?'

'What?'

'I can tell when something's going on.'

I groaned. 'Okay, Harry. You know I've met Katy Dark once before.'

'That's right. So you said.'

'What I didn't mention was that the meeting didn't quite go as expected. You know that photo of Katy? The skirt picture?'

'The skirt—' Harry stopped as realisation slowly spread across his face. 'You're *kidding*. That was *you*?'

I'd been an entertainment reporter back then. Most of my interviews had been with movie and television stars—and I'd spoken to some of the biggies over the years. The Melbourne paper I worked for had sent me to Sydney to interview Katy. Unfortunately, the flight had been late, and I'd driven like a madwoman to get to the hotel in time. Just as I arrived, I was dismayed to see Katy and her entourage leaving the hotel lobby.

I raced across the lobby. By then, Katy had headed up a flight of stairs to the mezzanine. When I started up after her, I stepped on her skirt.

'She was wearing this long, flowing thing,' I said. 'Horribly impractical. Anyway, I stepped on it, and she kept going. It got pulled down and...'

Well, if anyone had ever wondered what Katy Dark's bare butt looked like, they need wonder no longer. To make matters worse, a press photographer had taken a photo at that exact moment.

This had been published in just about every newspaper in Australia and even made the nightly news.

I blushed. I had a clumsiness gene, but it usually only affected me. This had affected Katy and her entire career. Maybe the worst part was the expression on Katy's face. After her initial astonishment, she'd turned with a look of utter fury. If looks could kill, I wouldn't have survived the day. Her security guard immediately formed a barrier between us as she pulled her skirt back up. Then Katy and her entourage had continued up the stairs, ignoring my desperate apologies.

Needless to say, I didn't get an interview.

Harry had contacted her publicist, Cindy Hillspring, and talked her into having a journalist around while Katy visited Cape Carson. My job was to keep a diary of events during her visit: places she went, people she met, how she spent her time.

Katy probably had no idea who they were sending. Had she known...

'She might not remember you,' Harry said gently. 'Even if she does, maybe she'll rise to the occasion. You know. Forgive and forget.'

'Maybe.'

I wasn't convinced.

'Of course,' Harry continued. 'This week, we've got the age-old news problem: there's either nothing happening, or everything's happening at once.'

'You mean the Cupcake Festival? And Spud Butler?'

Harry stroked his chin. 'The festival's one of the biggest events of the year. I've got Jay covering a lot of the stories.' Jay Patel, our junior reporter in the office, usually covered sports but was filling in while I shadowed Katy. 'And I'm quite busy at the moment with er...paperwork.' He pointed vaguely at some pages on his desk. 'There's only so much a man can do.'

'Okay.' Where was this going? I was already spending the week with Katy Dark as well as interviewing Spud Butler. 'Do you need help with something?'

'I was hoping you'd say that. Jay can handle the stories around the festival: the contest, the parade, and the world record attempt. So, if you can judge the Cupcake Contest, then I can—'

My jaw dropped. 'Wait a minute,' I interrupted. *Judge the Cupcake Contest?* Harry, I can't do that. You know what that's like!'

'Which is why we need a level headed individual—'

'Harry, if blood is going to be shed, it'll be over cupcakes.'

'All you need do is pick a winner.' Harry said it as if he were describing how to make a sandwich. 'I'd judge myself, but I've done it eight years running, and I feel the festival needs someone new.' He picked up some random pages. 'And I've got these...er, papers to look after.'

'Those are last month's fishing reports,' I said. 'Can't you find someone else? I'm not even in town.'

'You'll be at the lighthouse. It's two minutes up the road. You can hang out with Katy and then pop down to do a spot of judging.'

'Pop down to do a spot of judging?'

'You're making it sound like an onerous task.'

'Really? Because it's worse than onerous! I'd rather have my appendix taken out with a spoon! Don't you get death threats? Hate mail? Bribes?'

Harry waved away my concerns. 'Some people take it all a bit too seriously,' he said. 'You just need to remain true to your beliefs. Pick the entry you think deserves to win.' He leaned closer. 'Although, a word of advice. Try not to pick anyone you know.'

'Try not...' I stared at him. 'Harry. I know half the town.'

Harry sighed. 'I know,' he said. 'Good luck with that. By the way, the contest's at the Scout Hall again this year. I've rung the Cupcake Committee and told them you're dropping in today.'

'Really?' I said, frowning. 'You told them I'm dropping in? How did you know I'd agree to judge?'

'Because you can always be relied on to do what's right,' Harry said. 'That's why everyone loves you.'

Grumbling to myself, I went to my desk, where Jay and Ellie were speaking. Jay was holding out a plate of cupcakes to Ellie

Applegate, the twenty-two-year-old who looked after social media, advertising, and the paper's website.

'I'm not sure,' Ellie was saying.

'Not sure about what?' I asked, plonking down on my chair. I still had to finish a piece on the festival's history before leaving early for the day. Then I needed to meet with the Cupcake Committee and head home to pack a few things before joining Katy Dark's entourage.

Jay pointed to the cupcakes. 'My mother's been baking,' he said. 'She has finally perfected her recipe.'

'Oh?' The cupcakes were very yellow. 'What type are they?'

'Curry.'

'*Curry* cupcakes? You're kidding.'

'Not at all. They're nice. Try one.'

He offered the plate. It was a little early in the day for sweets, but I cautiously took a bite. 'That's...actually not too bad,' I said. 'In fact, it's pretty good.'

Encouraged by the fact that I hadn't fallen down dead, Ellie picked up one and tried it. 'Hmm,' she said. 'Surprisingly tasty.'

'Your mother may have redefined what a cupcake can be.' Ellie grabbed another cupcake and made good her escape as I turned to my computer. After a moment, I realised that Jay's gaze was still on me. 'Was there something else?'

'My mother would *love* to win the contest.'

'I'm sure she would.'

'She's asked if you'd like to come for dinner.'

That's odd, I thought. I'd met Jay's parents, but they'd never invited me to dinner before.

'Hang on,' I said, frowning. 'Did Harry tell you that I'm judging the cupcake contest?'

'He *might* have mentioned it. Anyway, Mum asked me to tell you about her cousin Aakesh. He's very wealthy and seeking a wife.'

I sat back from my desk. 'Jay,' I said. 'Is your mother trying to bribe me?'

'No!' Jay said. 'That would be...well...okay, it's a kind of bribe. But I met Aakesh when he came to Australia. He's very charming. Only twenty-four and just started as an engineer—'

'*Twenty-four?*' I groaned. 'I'm old enough to be his mother! And, Jay, I will not be bribed. The cupcake contest is supposed to unite the town in the spirit of friendly competition.'

'Really? My mother calls it a battle of survival with the weak being crushed underfoot while the strong prevail.'

'Well, she's...well...I'm busy.' I turned back to my computer. 'I've got to finish this story.'

'Sure,' Jay said, offering the plate again. 'Another?'

3

It ended up being a longer day than I'd expected.

I got out of the office just before three. From there, I headed down to the beach. Some days I just had to clear my head before I did anything else, and this was one of those times. Trixie tore past me and chased seagulls across the sand as I wandered along the coastal path. A tepid breeze blew in from the sea. The water was calm, and the sky above it, a sheet of turquoise blue. A fishing boat rounded the breakwater and arrowed for the fisherman's wharf.

I drew a deep breath.

This is the life.

I called to Trixie, and she came bouncing back. 'You're a naughty dog,' I admonished, laughing. 'Those seagulls will be forever scarred.'

She gave an answering bark before she glanced up the beach at a figure on the path.

I wasn't expecting to see you, I thought.

'Hey George,' I said.

My ex-husband nodded. His hands were sunk deep into his jacket, and he hadn't shaved. He'd put on weight too.

Considering he'd recently come back to live in Cape Carson, it was surprising that I hadn't seen him much.

'You busy?' he asked.

I wasn't sure if he meant *right at this moment* or *life in general,* so I just nodded. 'Lots of stuff's happening,' I said. 'You keeping okay?'

George nodded absently. 'Fine,' he said. 'Everything's great.'

'Really?' We'd been married a long time, and I could always tell when he was unhappy. 'You seem a little down.'

'It's nothing. Really.' He stopped. 'Blossom's in New South Wales.'

'For how long?' This sounded final. 'What's she doing there?'

'She's on a retreat with Madame Topaz.'

'Madame—who?'

'The woman specialises in healing harmonic vibration...I don't know...of gems or something.'

'Right.' I tried to feel glee at George's dismay. He had—after all—broken my heart and wrecked our twenty-year marriage. Yet, I couldn't muster up a feeling of hatred. All I felt was a little sad.

'Would you like to do dinner one night?' he asked.

'What?'

'Dinner? There's that Thai place? What's it called? Super Thai?'

It was the last place I wanted to go for a meal. Not only was it overpriced, but also a dive. Still, I didn't want to argue.

'Sure,' I said, trying to keep my voice neutral. 'When?'

We coordinated calendars and set a date. George headed off, and I went back up the road to my 2005 red Wrangler jeep. It was only as I climbed in, and Trixie had jumped in next to me, that I thought about what I'd just agreed to.

'Oh, Trixie,' I said. 'I can't believe I just did that. I'm going to dinner with George.'

Trixie barked.

'Is that a good bark or a bad bark?'

She barked again.

'I'll take it as bad,' I said. 'And I don't blame you one bit.'

My jeep started on its third attempt. I'd been having a few problems with it for a while. Well, *quite* a while.

I drove through town, turning onto Lennon Street, where the old Scout Hall sat nestled under gumtrees. The place was operating as the exhibition space for the cupcake contest.

It was a lovely big old building. My footsteps reverberated on the huon pine floorboards as I entered. Scouting paraphernalia hung on the walls: the Scout Promise, faded knot charts, photos of camps from years gone by, and maps of local bushwalking trails. Stored on the rafters above were battered canoes, tents, and boxes of dusty Christmas decorations.

The cupcake committee was huddled in what appeared to be an all too serious discussion. Wanda Gibson was the committee president. She had run the local library for thirty years before Kim took over as head librarian. Wanda had her arms crossed and was glaring at Sharon Costa, the wife of Giuseppe Costa, one of the area's biggest property developers. Sharon was a tall, buxom woman whereas Wanda was built like a bulldog. They could not have been more different.

The committee's third member was Reverend Raymond Tyler, the vicar from the Cape Carson Anglican Church. He was a small, twiglike man who had short-cropped grey hair and held his hands as if delivering a sermon.

'—reach agreement on the simple things,' he was saying. 'Then we can move on to more complex matters.'

'Complex!' Sharon snapped. 'We're talking about how to arrange tables in a hall.'

'They've *always* been laid out in a herringbone pattern,' Wanda replied. 'For the entire fifty-nine year history of the festival. Do you want to create a riot?'

'Really? Over the layout of tables?'

Reverend Tyler tried to intervene. 'Some people take these things quite seriously. They don't—'

'Rosie!' Wanda bellowed as she spotted me. 'So glad you're

here. We need the insight of a local with a discerning eye.'

The group bore down on me like a pack of hungry wolves.

Oh, dear.

'Now here is a real issue,' Sharon said. 'Nothing against you, Rosie, but I'm not sure you should be judging the contest.'

I was about to agree with her when Wanda cut me off.

'Why not?' Wanda demanded loudly. 'Rosie's a local and an intelligent woman to boot!'

'The judge should be a local,' Sharon said as if I weren't standing right in front of her. 'And Rosie's only a relative newcomer to the area.'

'But she did marry a local boy,' Wanda pointed out.

'But they're now divorced,' Sharon said.

'But her daughter Amanda is also a resident.'

'But Amanda did not grow up in the area.'

'But Amanda's husband Tom did and—'

'Ladies,' Reverend Tyler interrupted, conveying infinite blessings on them again. 'If we can stay focused on the table setup—'

'All right,' Sharon said, giving up. 'We'll have to take what we can get.'

'—although it is a shame Harry can't make it this year,' the Reverend continued. 'He's been such a good judge. There's no way he can be convinced?'

'He is experienced,' Wanda pointed out.

I stared at the three faces. The last thing I felt like doing was judging the Cupcake Contest. At the same time, I didn't like being kicked out of the job before I'd even started.

'Harry can't make it this year,' I said. 'He's...indisposed. Very busy with...things. I'm the judge, and I want to remind you that we're raising money for the local hospital.'

'Then we need a final word on the table layout,' Wanda said.

I glanced about the hall. 'It's usually in a herringbone?'

'It is.'

'Then you should stick with it.'

Wanda smiled. Sharon grimaced. Reverend Tyler shot a grateful look towards Heaven.

Sharon began. 'This town needs to get with the twenty-first century—'

'Anyway,' Wanda bulldozed over her loudly. 'A decision's been made, and we must abide. Rosie, do you have a copy of the manual?'

'Manual?'

'The Cupcake Judging manual. You can't judge without it.'

Taking my look of confusion as *no*, Wanda dove into her bag, dragged out a thick leather-bound folder and thrust it into my hands. A growing sense of dread enveloped me as I turned to page one. The contents page listed thirty-eight chapters with topics as diverse as texture, colour, flavour, moistness, sponginess, decorative value, and positivity index.

'What's this?' I asked as my gaze narrowed on a heading. '*Inappropriate Decorations*?'

'Cupcakes may not be adorned or topped with images of an offensive nature,' Wanda explained firmly. 'Section Fourteen. Paragraph nine.'

'What does that mean?' I asked, sitting the folder down. 'Exactly?'

'Three years ago, we had a young lady who entered cupcakes with images of, shall we say, parts of the body best kept behind closed doors.'

'Huh?'

Sharon smirked. 'Boobs.'

'I see.'

Reverend Tyler dived in. 'It's not just...er, inappropriate body imagery,' he said. 'But *any* imagery that is offensive.' He paused. 'I'll just say it: images of witchcraft should not be promoted.'

'Witches can be fun,' I said. 'At Halloween—'

'Oh, that's all light-hearted,' the reverend said, waving away my concerns. 'But some people are just trying to push their own agenda.'

'Which people?'

'Exactly. Witch people.'

I laughed, then realised Reverend Tyler was looking at me reproachfully.

'We have a group of witches in town,' he said, lowering his voice. 'A *coven*.'

'Really? I had no idea. I should interview them sometime.'

'Oh no! We don't want to promote them.'

Actually, they sounded like an intriguing topic for a story, but before I could express that opinion, my phone buzzed. I checked it: a reminder that I had to head home and pack before meeting Katy Dark. 'I'd better get moving,' I said, seizing the opportunity. 'You're all doing a wonderful job.'

'The folder,' Wanda said.

'Oh yes, the folder,' I said, grabbing the thing and wishing I could give it to the witches to burn in a sacrificial fire—or whatever they usually did. 'I'll be back for the judging. You're all doing well. Just put those tables out, and you're almost done.'

'And you know the judging time?'

She gave me the details and I dutifully entered them into my calendar.

'But if we have questions—' Reverend Tyler began.

'Just phone...I mean...*email* me.' It was bad enough having to judge the contest without having them ring me every five minutes. 'I'll get back to you.'

I raced back to my car with Trixie close behind. Settling in behind the wheel, I gritted my teeth.

Harry!

4

After pulling into the driveway of my home, I wearily made my way up the front steps and let myself in.

'Nan!' I announced. 'I'm back!'

My grandmother sat at the kitchen table, peering thoughtfully at a jigsaw puzzle. This was our latest household craze, and like so many others, would die off after a while. The three-thousand-piece puzzle was of the city of Rome as it would have looked in ancient times.

'How's it going?' I asked.

'Well,' Nan said. 'You know the old saying.'

I rolled my eyes. 'Not again.'

'Rome wasn't built in a day!'

'Yep. I'm sure.'

I'd only heard the joke about fifty million times already.

Nan indicated a nearby box. 'I've only just found my DVD collection,' she said. 'I was worried they might have been tossed out.'

'Collection of what?' I asked, grabbing a cold drink from the fridge.

'Horseshoe Farm.'

'What? You used to watch that show?'

'Religiously.' Nan frowned. 'What's wrong with that?'

'Er, it's just that it's a soap opera,' I said. 'You know, everyone gives each other long, lingering looks, and nobody speaks like regular people. It's always, *I could never love you, Penelope. I'm really in love with Gladiola.*'

'The show was nothing like that—and no one was named either Penelope or Gladiola. Anyway, I loved the character that Cameron Dark played.'

'Who was?'

'Cliff Granger.'

'See what I mean? How many people do you know named Cliff?'

'None.' She looked wistful. 'And there'll only ever be one Cliff for me.'

'Don't tell me you had a crush on Cameron Dark.'

'Are you kidding, girl? He was so hot he'd make ice melt. And who's calling the kettle black here? What's that horrible show you've been watching?'

I mumbled. '*Bogans in Love.*'

Nan burst out laughing. 'This is the show where toothless, unshaved blokes without shoes are dating supermodels?'

'They've got teeth. Mostly.'

Nan chuckled and asked if I'd get Cameron Dark to auto-graph her DVDs. I promised I'd try. Leaving Nan to fantasise about the two-legged stud of Horseshoe Farm, I headed to my room and grabbed my bag. I'd already packed most of my belongings for the weekend, but I still had to throw in my cosmetics. I'd just finished doing this when my phone beeped. Kim had sent me a message.

Have you met Chris yet? When can we accidentally meet on purpose?

I texted back.

No, I haven't met him. Maybe I can run him over in my jeep. You can happen to be passing by, give him mouth-to-mouth and be married by next week.

Kim texted back.

You're a cruel woman, Rosie Ryan.

I wrote back, laughing.

I know.

Nan's boyfriend Dave had arrived by the time I lugged my bag back to the living room. His car—a black 1970's Valiant with flames down the side—was parked out the front. When I first met Dave, I wasn't sure how to take him, although I soon worked out that he was a good guy. I wasn't sure what would happen between him and Nan. She was eighty-three, and he was seventy-seven.

Still, they seemed to enjoy each other's company.

'Hey Rosie,' Dave said. He had short-cropped grey hair, a boxed beard, and murky tattoos on both arms. 'Nan tells me you're hanging with the stars.'

'Something like that.' I explained that I was covering Katy Dark and Spud Butler while they were in town.

'Spud Butler,' Dave mused. 'Personally, I prefer the older crowd of country singers: Smokey Dawson, Reg Lindsay. Still, these younger guys aren't bad.' He frowned. 'And that Katy Dark woman...Isn't she working on some new movie? Something about a robot protecting the President?'

'That's right.' I'd read about it while doing background research. '*The President's Robot*.' I turned to Nan. 'Should I get Katy's autograph as well?'

'Don't bother. I've never forgiven her for stealing Cameron from me.'

I laughed. 'I don't think it's quite like that.'

'He only left Horseshoe Farm because of that woman. She wanted them to spend more time together.' Nan grimaced, annoyed that true love could derail her favourite TV show. 'They had him run over by a combine harvester. Terrible way to kill him off.'

'It's a soap,' I said. 'It could turn out that someone else got crushed by the harvester. Maybe Ridge Johnson...or Butt Naked...or someone. And Cliff can come out of hiding to track down the killer.'

'Now you're just being silly.' She stopped thoughtfully. 'You're staying at the Lighthouse Inn, aren't you?'

I nodded.

'Sheila Birdwhistle runs that place. We used to go dancing years ago. She's a good lady. Could talk the leg off a chair, but kind-hearted. Give her my best.'

Promising I would, I said goodbye to Nan and Dave, headed to the car with Trixie, and drove off. I felt a sense of growing trepidation as we passed through town. Would Katy Dark remember that I was the person who stepped on her skirt? And if she did, what would she do? Punch me in the nose? Throw me out of the inn?

My heart was in my throat by the time I reached my lodgings. The bluestone building sat in a small glade just behind the Cape Carson Lighthouse at Carr's Promontory.

Built originally as the lighthouse keeper's home, the place was transformed into an inn when the lighthouse was decommissioned in 1986. Its transformation since then included a tacky redbrick extension, a timber bungalow, and a shed out the back.

However, none of this took much away from the lighthouse. It was still the tallest structure in Cape Carson, the gallery at the top providing the most spectacular view on this part of the coast.

The lighthouse was the town's leading tourist attraction; there probably wasn't a holidaymaker to Cape Carson who didn't stop by.

Pulling into the car park, I noted the prestige vehicles already in residence: a BMW, Alfa Romeo, Audi. My old banged-up jeep looked like it was ready for the scrapyard. I turned to Trixie. 'I refuse to feel ashamed because of my car,' I said. 'This old jeep is my pride and joy.'

Trixie whined.

'I knew you'd agree,' I said.

Giving the dashboard a last pat, I got out, grabbed my bags, and made my way into the building. A plump woman with a mop of untidy blonde hair and a printed flower dress stood behind the counter.

We introduced ourselves.

Sheila continued brightly. 'And before you ask, I know nothing about birds or whistles. How's your Nan? She's a remarkable woman. And you, too. All that business about the old Bailey house and ghosts. It amazes me you survived the whole thing. And that's your car out there? What a classic—'

Sheila seemed able to speak despite not drawing breath. I was reminded of people who could play the bagpipes.

I cut in. 'So I've got a room?'

'You have indeed. A lovely room. Well, they're all lovely, but this one has a beautiful view of the trees out the side. The biggest one was planted by Edward Carr himself. He was the first lighthouse keeper. Did you know that? I suppose most people—'

As she continued to speak, I turned my attention to the displays behind the counter.

It was like visiting a nautical museum. There was an ancient sea chart. A whaling harpoon. A barometer and compass. And a key that seemed to take pride of place.

'That's the key to the lighthouse?' I asked.

'It is. Still works too, Rosie. The Australian Maritime Safety Authority originally managed the lighthouse, but these days it's the Cape Carson Historical Society. They've got their own key, but this one's the original—'

'That's so interesting,' I said, cutting in. 'And Nan says *hi*. I'll head up to my room. Have Katy and Cameron arrived yet?'

'Not yet. How lucky are we to have someone like Katy Dark staying! Imagine that! Katy Dark! And her husband. I did love him in Horseshoe Farm. Lovely man. Lovely.'

Scooping up my key, I thanked Sheila again and dragged my luggage up the stairs with Trixie trailing behind. I was in the first room on the left. A neatly painted One decorated the door. Opening the door revealed a cosy, light chamber with the usual set pieces: a bed, nightstand, wardrobe, and ensuite bathroom. I'd stayed in a hundred similar places over the years.

I didn't have a view of the lighthouse. Actually, I didn't have a view of anything. Only the tree outside of which Sheila had sung its praises. I had no idea if it had really been planted by Edward Carr, but it was a pretty ordinary tree that only served to block my view. Leaning out, I could make out a section of the headland, the place where it turned towards a spot called Mermaid Point, and beyond it, seven uninterrupted miles of sand known as West Beach.

I hung my clothing in the wardrobe. Contained within was a tiny chest of drawers and, beside this, a shoebox-sized metal safe bolted to the floor. The combination and safe door were set into the top.

Large enough to hold all my valuables, I thought. *Because I don't have any!*

I heard the murmur of voices. It was low at first, but one was quickly raised in irritation. Easing open my door, I saw a woman speaking to Sheila.

'—must be able to give me a better room.' The woman was small and stout and wore round glasses. Her frizzy black hair was salted with grey. 'I was promised a good view.'

Sheila looked uncomfortable. 'That's the best we can do under the circumstances,' she said. 'Katy Dark has the View Room. It's the best room in the hotel, and all the other rooms have already been allocated.'

'But it's not quite right,' the woman said and then spotted me. 'Oh, hello.'

'Hi there,' I said and introduced myself.

Trixie barked, and the woman gave her a brief smile.

'Charlotte Bannister,' the woman said. 'I'm trying to sort out my room. It's not what I needed.'

Needed?

'Was expecting,' Charlotte corrected herself. 'I was hoping for a view.'

There was a sound on the stairs, and a man appeared. He was fortyish and attractive, and I recognised him immediately. This was the famous Chris Dawson, the man that Kim had enjoyed that golden summer with many years before. Kim had shown me a picture that she'd found of him on social media, and he'd changed little. Lean, with a square jaw, he looked more like a movie star himself than an author.

More introductions followed before Chris pushed open the door to room Seven on the opposite side of the hall and glanced in. His gaze went to the window and the view beyond.

'He's just booked in,' Charlotte said. 'Why can't I have his room?'

'All the rooms were allocated weeks ago,' Sheila said. 'And that wouldn't be fair.'

'I don't mind,' Chris said. 'Happy to be accommodating.'

'Are you sure—' Sheila began.

Charlotte cut in. 'That's so kind,' she enthused, seizing the opportunity to squeeze past us and into the room. The door closed firmly behind her.

Sheila sighed. 'Well,' she said. 'As long as everyone's happy.'

5

I finished unpacking before going downstairs to explore the rest of the building.

Although living in Cape Carson for five years, I'd visited the lighthouse several times, but never the inn.

The upper floor was part of the modern extension, as was most of downstairs. It was the west end of the building that was original, with the office, reception, and what appeared to be Sheila's living quarters.

These rooms were cramped with roughhewn, whitewashed stone walls and tiny square windows. I passed through a door to the opposite side of the building. This was more expansive: a commercial kitchen, library, study, and a dining room with picture windows that faced the ocean and town. The dining room looked like it usually accommodated separate groups, but now the tables and seating had been drawn together for a dinner party.

Inside the inn's kitchen, the chef was busy chopping kale.

A young guy, maybe twenty-two with dark hair and a build reminiscent of a lightweight boxer, was prepping at such a pace it made me feel like I'd never spent a day in the kitchen. A girl, aged about eighteen, was folding napkins.

She glanced up to see Trixie and me in the entryway. 'Good afternoon,' she said. 'Can I help you?'

'No. We were just taking a look around.'

After saying hello to Trixie, the girl introduced herself as Dorothy Stuart and the chef as Jason Rodd. She explained that she was the assistant manager. However, I suspected her role equated to doing everything Mrs Birdwhistle didn't want to do. I studied the girl's face. She was lovely, with dark hair and startling grey eyes.

'Dinner's at six-thirty,' Dorothy explained. 'Katy Dark and her husband should be here by then.'

I nodded, feeling that same sense of trepidation. This could be a very unpleasant dinner if Katy recognised me. I turned to leave.

'Oh!' I said, walking straight into someone. 'So sorry!'

The man laughed. 'Don't worry about it,' he said. 'I've got a habit of creeping up on people.'

He was an older man, balding with a white handlebar moustache. I recognised him immediately.

'You're Colin Wood?' I said.

'Guilty as charged.' The man seemed perpetually cheerful.

'And you are?'

I introduced myself, saying that I'd been an entertainment reporter in Melbourne, but not mentioning that infamous occasion when we'd first met. Fortunately, back then, I'd been living under my married name of Lazaridis.

'I'm here to cover Katy's visit to town,' I explained, keen to not dwell on anything that might reflect the past. 'You're still Katy's manager?'

'Ex-manager,' Colin said after the briefest hesitation. 'We parted ways a while back, but we're still on good terms. She invited me to stay for the weekend.'

'Pleased to hear it.'

'I hear that you've already met Chris.'

I said that I had. Colin invited me to join him and Chris on the front veranda for a drink. After Dorothy poured me a soft drink, I joined the men outside.

'Look who I bumped into,' Colin said. 'Literally!'

I settled into a metal-framed garden chair opposite Chris and Colin. I tried to envision Kim and Chris experiencing first love at the beach when they were teenagers. Oddly, it wasn't hard to imagine.

Chris Dawson, despite his good looks, had a slightly boyish appearance. Kim, although the same age as me, easily looked younger. I wondered if anything could be rekindled between them. He bent over and patted Trixie. 'You do any writing other than journalism?' Chris asked.

'I'm trying to write a book,' I said. 'But I haven't gotten very far in. Anyway, my work for the Gazette keeps me busy.'

'Really?'

'There's always something to cover. We've got the Annual Cupcake Festival this week.'

'Oh, right.' Chris raised an eyebrow. 'And *that's* news?'

I could feel my face reddening. 'Oh, it's...news-*ish*,' I said. 'But there are always things happening.'

'Like what?' Colin asked.

Despite having written thousands of articles for the Gazette, I couldn't think of a single item that counted as news. *What have I been doing for the last five years? Think of something. Think!* Bizarrely, the only news item I could think of concerned a two hundred thousand dollar renovation of the local public toilets. It seemed an exorbitant amount to spend on dunnies. If I spent that on my home bathroom, the place would be clad in gold.

I desperately tried to think of some way to change the topic. 'Well,' I said, an idea popping magically into my brain. 'You know what Cape Carson's like.'

Chris looked confused. 'What makes you say that?'

'Oh,' I said, realising the blunder I'd made. 'Someone...a person I know...mentioned they knew you.'

'Really? Who?'

I felt like a deer caught in the headlights, except getting run over by a semi-trailer would have been a blessing. 'Um. Kim?' I said weakly.

'Kim?'

'Kim Chen.'

'Kim Chen?' he said. 'She still lives here?'

I nodded, thinking, *I've made a complete mess of this*, and turned to Colin in a desperate hope he might somehow steer the conversation in another direction.

Instead, he was staring at me too. 'Rosie,' he said, frowning. 'You mentioned being an entertainment reporter. So we've met before?'

'No,' I said. 'Yes...I...no. Well, you know how things are. Ships in the night. Passing flings. I mean...I don't mean *flings*, exactly.' Colin was now staring at me, possibly wondering if he'd ever seen me unclothed. 'We've never...'

At that moment, a black BMW SUV pulled into the car park.

'Oh, look!' I said, desperate for a diversion. 'A car.'

'Yes,' Chris said, dourly. 'Thrilling.'

The SUV stopped beside my vehicle, making my beloved red Wrangler jeep look all the more like something that had been dumped on the street. The driver, a muscled man with a shaved head, climbed from the driver's seat and made his way around to the passenger side. The door opened, and Katy Dark stepped out.

Katy wore sunglasses and a slim-fitting red dress and carried a pug in her hands. She settled him on the ground, and he went racing around the car until Katy called him back. Cameron Dark got out the other side of the vehicle. He was much taller than her and astonishingly good-looking. I could see why Nan loved him so much. Katy scooped up her dog and gave him a kiss. He barked happily, and Trixie wagged her tail.

I patted Trixie's head.

Friendship might not be a possibility, I thought. *We'll have to see.*

The driver, who I suspected was also Katy's bodyguard, went to the boot, took out a couple of bags, and carried them with ease as they headed for the inn.

'The Queen has arrived,' Colin murmured.

I glanced at him. *What's that supposed to mean?* Maybe his split with her hadn't been as amicable as Colin had suggested. Reaching the veranda, Katy's eyes took in Chris and Colin before settling on me.

'*Ah ha,*' she said. 'Rosie Lazaridis!'

My heart sank as the actress arrowed towards me. Despite being taller and bigger than her, I still felt like a child about to receive punishment.

I'd rehearsed a speech for this eventuality, but now it flew straight out of my head. Only one clear thought went through my mind.

I know what your butt looks like!

'Rosie,' Katy said, removing her glasses. 'It's so lovely to see you.'

'Huh?'

'I owe you so much.'

'Huh?'

'You must remember? Stepping on my skirt? It was the best thing that ever could have happened. It couldn't have been a better promotional opportunity if we'd arranged it.' She turned to Colin. 'Possible we should have hired Rosie full-time?'

Colin grinned. 'Of course!' he said. 'That's where I know you from! The famous skirt incident!' He shook his head in admiration. 'How lucky were we?'

Huh?

Then all the pieces slowly came together. Of course, that photo had been everywhere: newspapers, television, and social media. Millions of people saw it. *Millions.* There had to be some commercial advantage to that.

Finally rediscovering my voice, I glanced down at Katy's dress. 'No skirt today.'

'I'll have to find some other way to make the news.' She nodded vigorously. 'But thank goodness you're an R.'

'An R?'

She smiled. 'R for Rosie,' she said. 'Most everyone else is a C. There's Cameron, of course. But then we've got Chris and Colin, and then there's Chadek, our security guard. And my publicist, Cindy—Lord knows where's she's gone—who is another C!'

By now, her dog was squirming with excitement in her arms at the sight of Trixie.

'Of course, Garry's not a C,' said Katy, holding up her dog. 'We love Rosie. Don't we, Garry? And who's this?'

'Trixie.'

'What a beautiful beagle,' she said.

She put him down, and the dogs gave each other a good sniffing.

'There they are,' Katy said. 'Friends already.' She pointed to her husband. 'I don't know if you've met Cameron.'

Cameron Dark smiled and gave me a warm handshake. His eyes were grey and clear. I'd gotten into the habit of examining the eyes of people in film and television. It was to see if they were on drugs, but it seemed the only high he and Katy were on was fame.

'So pleased to meet you, Rosie,' he said. 'Your reputation precedes you.'

'Thanks,' I said. 'Nice to know I'm famous for something.'

Katy burst out laughing again. It all seemed over the top, but I suppose being an international star gave her a lot to laugh about. She headed inside with Cameron, Chris, and Colin in her wake, leaving me behind with the driver.

'I'm Rosie,' I said.

'Chadek Ivanov.'

With a name and accent like that, he had to be Russian. I wondered what he'd done before working for Katy. His physique was more like a boxer than a wrestler; he knew how to look after himself.

How does a Russian tough guy end up working for someone like Katy Dark?

'You're Katy's bodyguard?'

'Bodyguard,' he said, shrugging. His English was good. Not perfect, but good. Despite a deep guttural ring to his voice, he enunciated his words clearly enough. 'Driver, dog walker...'

I wasn't sure if he was making a joke or not. Probably not. There was something in my research about Katy's bodyguard. The memory hovered beyond reach.

What was it?

We trailed in after the group. Katy and Cameron had been formally met by Sheila Birdwhistle and Dorothy Stuart. The younger girl seemed instantly enamoured by Cameron; her eyes were fixed on him. I could understand why. He was one of those rare individuals blessed with rugged, handsome looks: the classic soap star.

But it was more than that.

Cameron seemed physically bigger than himself. Almost as if his presence emanated beyond him. Although now the more famous of the two, Katy Dark seemed slight by comparison.

Sheila was speaking. '...the View Room, which is our very best,' she was saying. 'It's the largest room and has the best outlook in the whole building. There's a safe in the wardrobe in your room. I can come up and show you if you like.'

'That won't be necessary,' Cameron said.

'And I've arranged for a tour of the lighthouse,' Sheila said.

'Wonderful,' Katy replied.

'Sunset is in an hour. It's the best time to take in the view.'

'Of course.'

The group headed upstairs to unpack, leaving me with Sheila and Dorothy. I felt relieved at how things had turned out. Katy hadn't punched me in the nose. She actually seemed pleased to see me.

'Wow,' Dorothy said. 'So, that's Katy Dark.'

'She certainly is,' Sheila confirmed. 'And she's brought the Horizon Ring with her.'

6

'Really?' I said. 'The Horizon Ring?'

'That's what her publicist woman told me,' Sheila said. 'What's her name? Cindy Hillspring?'

'Isn't that kind of risky?'

'There's a safe in her room. It'd take dynamite to open.'

I nodded thoughtfully. Still, it was risky. The Horizon Ring wasn't priceless, but it was worth millions. The diamond was a fifteen-carat blue emerald cut diamond set into a gold ring. Katy had inherited it from an aunt in South Africa who ran a diamond mine. A photo of Katy Dark wearing the ring had made it to the front page of one of the women's magazines.

This was an interesting angle. No longer was the story *Katy Dark Visits Cape Carson*, but *Movie Star Visits with Rare Diamond*.

I decided to change my shoes to climb the lighthouse. Reaching the top of the stairs, I spotted Katy in the doorway of her room opposite mine. She was deep in conversation with

Chris.

'...should have the book finished in the next three months,' Chris was saying.

That's right, I remembered. *Chris is helping Katy to write her autobiography.*

I wondered what that really meant. Ghostwriters often did the writing, and the celebrity took all the credit. I went into my room, swapped shoes, and headed back to the hallway with Trixie just as the grandfather clock chimed five.

That's an old clock, I thought. *I wonder how often it chimes.*

A door down the corridor opened, and Cameron appeared. I stored away this piece of trivia: Katy and Cameron weren't sharing a room. Then Charlotte appeared from the next room. Her jaw dropped open at the sight of Cameron.

He probably has that effect on a lot of women.

The last door on the same side opened, and Chadek stepped out. I frowned. Considering he was Katy's bodyguard, it was a little surprising that he wasn't situated closer to her.

Although, I thought. *He can't be expected to be at Katy's side twenty-four hours a day.*

Downstairs, I found Sheila still at the front desk and asked her about the grandfather clock.

'That was brought over by Edward Carr from Scotland,' Sheila said. 'It chimes every hour on the hour. I'm proud to say it's been running more or less continuously for the last hundred and fifty years.'

Nodding, I headed to the front veranda where Colin and a woman were speaking. This was obviously Cindy Hillspring. I'd never met Cindy in person.

She looked forty and was gangly like a teenager, with dry, straw-coloured hair. My first impression was that of a mouse, which was surprising. Most publicists were loud and pushy, as their job was to trumpet their client's interests. Cindy struck me as someone who'd prefer to hide in the corner.

She glanced around, noticing me. 'Sorry about that,' she said. 'Business. You're Rosie Ryan?'

'Nice to finally meet you,' I said, shaking her hand.

'Ditto. Always happy to make ourselves available to the press.'

What a load of rubbish. Celebrities usually only spoke to the press when they wanted to promote a new project.

Charlotte arrived at that moment, and Cindy stared as if she didn't recognise the woman. Then she stirred. 'Charlotte,' she said. 'Congratulations on winning the contest. You must be excited to meet Katy.'

'Oh, yes,' Charlotte responded. 'Absolutely.'

Cindy asked if Charlotte had seen many of Katy's movies, and Charlotte said she'd seen them all at least three times. They chatted for another minute until Katy and the others arrived on the veranda. Katy had Garry under her arm. I wondered if she ever let him run around free.

'Katy,' Cindy said. 'This is Charlotte, the winner of the Women's Life contest. She's joining us for the weekend.'

Katy laughed. 'Another *C*,' she said, explaining about the number of people whose names began with the letter. 'So pleased to have you along, although I don't know why anyone would want to spend the weekend with me.'

'You're a wonderful actress.'

'You're joining us for the tour?' Cameron said.

'Absolutely. I love lighthouses.'

Charlotte chatted to Cameron as we made our way along the path from the inn to the lighthouse. It only took a few minutes. I'd walked to the Cape Carson Lighthouse a hundred times over the last few years, but it was interesting doing it as a tourist. When everyone wasn't *oohing* and *aahing* about the building and the beauty of the coastline, they were sharing their own lighthouse stories.

Colin mentioned that one of his ancestors had been a lighthouse keeper. The man had worked on the famed Southerness Lighthouse on the southwest coast of Scotland. Laughing, Cameron mentioned one of his first acting jobs was a bit part where he had to lug someone's scientific gear up the stairs to the top.

'I had to drag the bags up and down the stairs for three days so they could get two minutes of film,' he said. 'It was *not* what

I thought acting was about.'

Some late walkers noticed Katy and Cameron and whipped out phones to take pictures. Chadek made to block them, but Katy waved him away.

'Always available for a selfie,' she said loudly.

I noticed Cameron standing quietly at one side while Katy posed with Garry. The tourists had no interest in getting their pictures taken with Cameron.

Horseshoe Farm was a long time ago, I thought. *And Katy's star is on the rise.*

The tour guide was waiting at the front door to the lighthouse. He introduced himself as Ken and warned people it was thirty-two metres to the top. Anyone with heart problems should stay behind. After a short silence, no one admitted to health issues, and we started up.

Katy was immediately behind Ken as we ascended, and I remembered Colin's comment about her being the queen. I couldn't help but feel like I was part of her royal party. I glanced back and saw that Charlotte was still in deep conversation with Cameron. *She really is taken by him.* Now that I thought about it, Katy had not shown the slightest affection towards her husband.

Ken explained various parts of the lighthouse as we went. The first floor was a storeroom. The second level had living quarters with bunks and built-in robes. The floor above was a service area that opened onto the lamp room. The stairs narrowed as we ascended, and we jammed in together as Ken pointed out the light's components.

'In the early days,' he began, 'the light was produced using vapourised kerosene. In 1923, they started using acetylene, and then electricity in 1973. Eventually, the lighthouse was decommissioned in 1986 when a new lighthouse was constructed further up the coast. That one is fully automated.'

Stepping to one side, he opened the door to the main gallery balcony outside.

The wind pushed against my face as I followed the others. Everyone went out except for Chris, whose gaze was focused on the light. He had his back turned to the view and was asking Ken how the turning mechanism worked.

I took a deep breath. The sky was clear and the sea calm. Seagulls wheeled around the cliff below. A freighter inched across the distant horizon. Closer in, a sailboat tacked through the calm water.

My phone beeped: Kim.

Have you met Chris yet? What's he like?

I sent back a quick text.

He's great. He'd marry you, but he's already married with twelve children.

She wrote back.

I hate you.

Laughing, I put my phone away. Ken had continued to speak about the lighthouse's history, but I don't think anyone was listening. It was peaceful, and everyone was focused on their own thoughts. Even Katy seemed content as she stared out at sea. I studied her face. Being up here seemed to have momentarily stripped something away. Maybe the presence of fame. Up here, as she stared out at the water, she was just another person enjoying the view.

On impulse, I snapped a picture of her. I don't think she even noticed.

Finally, Ken said it was time to head back down again. Chris had become entranced by the mechanics of how the light worked. He hadn't even bothered to come out to enjoy the view. Everyone trailed down the stairs and back to the inn.

Returning to my room, my stomach was growling as I changed for dinner. I could hear the murmur of voices from down the hall. Easing my door open a crack, I peered out to see the publicist, Cindy, speaking to Cameron. Her hand was on his arm. There was something about the way they stood together that set my senses tingling.

There was something very *intimate* in their closeness.

I don't think all is well in Katy Dark's marriage.

But how was that possible? Katy was a gorgeous film star, and Cindy was…well, plain to put it nicely. A bit scrawny, if anything. And Cameron had an almost otherworldly handsomeness to him. Still, maybe he saw beyond her appearance. They obviously spent a lot of time on the road together.

Perhaps romance had blossomed in the background while Katy took centre stage.

I closed the door. My phone rang, and I glanced at the caller. 'Hey Todd,' I said. 'What can I do for you?'

'Just wanted to hear a friendly voice.'

'Really?' As much as I liked Todd, he usually didn't call me to chat. 'Tough day at the office?'

'Kind of. I had to break up a fight.'

'At the pub?'

'No. Mimi's Textile Bar. Two women both wanted the same fabric to finish their Cupcake parade outfits. One ended up with a black eye, and the other's got a sprained wrist.'

'Fabric's serious business,' I said. 'And the Cupcake Parade's one of the biggest events of the year. Everyone likes to either be in it or watching it.'

There was a pause. 'One of the women mentioned that she's getting dressed up as a cupcake,' Todd said.

'And?'

'A cupcake,' Todd repeated as if I hadn't heard him the first time. 'You know, a small cake with icing—'

'I know what a cupcake is, Todd. Lots of people dress up as cupcakes for the parade.'

Silence.

I continued. 'Okay, maybe people do take things a bit too seriously—'

'Like black eyes and sprained wrists.'

'—but everyone's got their quirks. And I don't hassle you because you drive around in a police car with flashing lights and a siren.'

'The lights are very pretty,' Todd teased me. 'And the siren's great fun. You can try it out sometime if you like.'

I laughed. 'You can keep your siren,' I said. 'But mark my word. Things will get a whole lot dirtier before they get better.'

'I don't doubt it.' He asked me how things were going with Katy and the gang.

'Well, everything seems fine—on the surface.'

'And below?'

I told him about seeing Cindy and Cameron in the hallway. 'It's not just them,' I said. 'There's an odd tension in the air. I'm not sure what it is. The only ones who seem to be having any real fun are Katy and Garry.'

'Garry?'

'Her pug.'

Todd groaned. 'Oh no,' he said. 'Not a pug.'

'Huh?'

'Better you than me. They're the one dog I can't stand.'

'Really? Pugs?'

'It's their squishy faces. It's like they ran into too many

walls.'

'Great,' I said. 'Now I know what to get you for Christmas.'

Todd said, *don't you dare* and hung up. I headed downstairs to the dining room to find everyone—except Katy—standing around chatting. The Queen obviously liked to make a grand entrance.

I wonder what tonight will bring.

7

The dinner was lovely.

I had chicken cacciatore, a favourite dish of mine, and this turned out to be the best I'd ever eaten. Everyone else seemed to enjoy their meals too. Katy had the same as me. Charlotte and Cameron chose the lobster mornay. Cincy, Colin, and Chris all ordered lasagne. The only odd one who chose classic Australian cuisine was Chadek, who had steak and chips.

I gazed around the table, thinking of all the C's. It sounded like a nineteen-fifties rock band: *The Six Cees*. Katy and I and the Lighthouse Inn staff were the only interlopers whose names didn't begin with that letter.

Oddly, during the meal, I found it hard to focus. Maybe it was boredom. In fact, I'm sure it was boredom. This was a group of people I didn't know well, and I didn't care to know. In essence, I'd been invited to a stranger's party and felt left out.

My mind kept returning to my family and friends. Nan

would be at home with Dave, probably working on the jigsaw puzzle of Rome. Next door, Amanda and Tom were probably sharing an evening together. Maybe watching some TV.

George would be at home with his brother, Nico, most likely playing a computer game that involved guns and zombies. I'd seen Nico around Cape Carson a few times of late. Like George, he worked as a plumber, but unlike George, he was rough-looking and skinny with a blonde ponytail. He really seemed to have gone downhill the last few years.

And what about Todd? He lived alone. Well, not completely alone. He had his three-legged greyhound dog, Rocko.

I wondered what it would be like to sit nestled before the television, maybe eating takeout with Todd's arm looped around my shoulder.

I kind of liked the idea. At least, I preferred it to this. There was nothing too extraordinary about this get-together.

Nothing except for...

'Katy,' I said. 'I hope you don't mind me mentioning it, but that's quite a lump of rock on your finger.'

Katy burst out laughing and held out her hand. 'It's hard to miss,' she admitted.

The Horizon Ring was a sight to behold. The stone was a sparkling blue rectangle that ran lengthways along her ring finger. Somehow, the four delicate white gold claws securely held the stone in place. Katy let me snap a few pictures, and I got a perfect one of her hand in the foreground with her face behind.

'There's nothing else quite like it on Earth,' Cameron said. 'Katy's lucky to have it.'

'It must be worth a lot,' I said.

'We only just had it revalued. It would be crass to say how much the valuation came in at, but we could sell it and most probably buy a small country with the proceeds.'

'On that note,' Katy said, 'I'll return the ring to the safe. Even I get worried about wearing it out.'

She nodded to Chadek, and they left the room, returning a few minutes later to continue the conversation.

'You must worry about security,' I said.

'For the ring? No, Rosie. Not really. It rarely leaves our safe in Melbourne. And Chadek always comes with us when we travel.'

I turned to the bodyguard. 'I imagine you can handle yourself.'

Chadek eyed me carefully. 'You just need to be ready.'

Charlotte spoke up. 'Maybe robbery is the least of your worries,' she said. 'It must be quite dangerous when you're protecting a famous person. I mean, there are crazy people out there.' She turned to Katy. 'Aren't you worried about stalkers?'

The actress laughed, but Cameron looked serious. 'There *are* dangerous people about,' he said. 'Not a week goes by that we don't hear from some crackpot. We've already had an incident today.'

'Cameron,' Katy said, a warning note in her voice.

He ignored her. 'There was a note on the front counter,' he said. 'When we got back from the lighthouse.'

'A note?' I repeated. 'You mean a threatening letter? What did it say?'

'Nothing,' Katy said. 'Just another crackpot. There's a few around.'

'But how did they get in?'

Cindy spoke up. 'The front door was open,' she said. 'I've spoken to Sheila, and she's agreed to keep it locked while Katy's here.'

'That should have been the case anyway,' Cameron Dark grumbled.

'We are guests here,' Katy said carefully. 'And we're ready now. We've got our eyes open. Everything's fine. And Chadek can handle anyone who gets out of hand.'

'That can cause problems in itself,' Colin murmured.

It was an odd comment.

What does he mean?

Chadek spoke up. 'There are people who...how do you say...step over the line,' he said. 'They should not do that.'

The penny dropped. This was what had been teasing my memory earlier. 'Didn't someone's arm get broken?' I asked.

Cameron shot me a look, and I instantly regretted speaking. *Well, bad luck. The cat's out of the bag now.* 'There was a fan? A woman?'

'At Sydney airport,' Chadek said. 'She ran at Katy, waving a box. I took care of the woman.'

Colin snorted. 'Seems like a funny way to take care of someone,' he said. 'Breaking her arm.'

I had the feeling this wasn't the first time this conversation had happened.

'The box could have contained anything,' Chadek said. 'A bomb. A snake. Acid.'

'So what was it?' I asked.

'It was a homemade jewellery box,' Katy said. 'We made restitution to the woman. That's old news.'

Katy had a fantastic ability to deliver unreadable looks, and she gave me that expression now. I'd seen that lock in one of her movies—*The Wife Next Door*. She'd played a psychopath who killed her neighbour so she could have her husband. When asked about the murder, her expression had been blank, almost like looking at static.

It was oddly unnerving. No one spoke for a moment. Then—

'Rosie's also a writer,' Colin said, breaking the ice.

'Really?' Cameron said. 'What do you write, Rosie?'

Laughing, I told them about my novel—if it could be called

that. Mostly, it was a few dozen pages of story that went nowhere. Chris had the good grace to say that novel writing was a lot harder than it looked.

'I've always wanted to write a book,' Charlotte piped up.

'Really?' I replied. 'What genre?'

'Romance.'

Katy spoke. 'There's always a market for romance,' she said, giving Cameron a sideways look. 'People love to see others happy.'

Cameron did not return the look.

'I've started on the book a few times,' Charlotte said, seemingly oblivious to the cold war taking place between Cameron and Katy. 'I just can't seem to make the characters work.'

'Well, I certainly don't know anything about writing novels,' I said. 'That's Chris' speciality.'

He gave a small smile. 'Fiction isn't my thing,' he said. 'I've co-written several biographies. It's a system that works.'

Katy laughed. 'Chris's been my saving grace,' she said. 'He inspires me to keep writing. If it were just up to me, the book would never be done.'

I wondered who was really doing the writing: Chris or Katy. Most likely, it was Chris. That's usually how the process worked. 'How far in are you?' I asked, trying to direct the question at both of them.

'Almost done,' Chris said. 'Just some minor editing now.'

Dessert arrived, and the conversation moved onto other topics. Although everyone seemed friendly, I sensed the same odd tension that I'd noticed earlier. What was it? Clearly, it originated around Katy. Maybe no one wanted to step on her toes. So what did that make everyone? Sycophants?

Maybe. I suppose I was, too, in my own way. I wanted a story for the Gazette. Charlotte was here because she'd wanted to meet Katy. Cindy was paid to be here. So were Chadek and Chris. Colin was once her manager. He wasn't here to relive old times. Maybe he was hoping to reclaim his previous position.

And Cameron? Well, he may have been Katy's husband, but they clearly weren't happily married. It may have been a marriage of convenience, or maybe he'd loved her once, and that was now over.

The rest of the evening passed with people talking about what kind of novels they would like to write—if they could ever put pen to paper. Cameron thought he could write a thriller. Cindy was also interested in romance. Chadek and Colin thought they could produce adventure stories.

Katy surprised everyone by saying she'd like to try her hand at science-fiction.

'It's what I read when I need to relax,' she said. 'It's lovely to be involved in something out of this world.'

Just before eleven o'clock arrived, Colin glanced at his watch and said he was heading to bed. I stayed to finish my drink before heading upstairs soon after. Here, Colin stood at the end of the hallway, gazing out the window.

Hope Colin wasn't waiting for me, I thought. *He's not my type.*

'Enjoy the party?' he asked.

'It's fine. And you?'

'I've been to Katy's parties a hundred times over. They're always the same. They'll carry on for another hour, and then everyone goes to bed drunk and unhappy. Katy won't make another appearance till late tomorrow morning. She's always a late riser.' He glanced out the window. 'It's a lovely night for a stroll.'

I feigned a yawn. 'It's way past my bedtime, I'm afraid.'

Wishing him goodnight, I headed into my room as the grandfather clock in the hallway chimed. *11.00pm.* I hoped it wouldn't keep me awake all night. After getting changed, I climbed into bed and lay in the dark, listening. The murmur of voices, plus the occasional burst of laughter, floated up the stairs. I was almost asleep when my phone pinged: Kim.

Are you awake?

I messaged back.

No. I'm asleep.

The phone rang a second later.

'It's me,' Kim said.

'Really? I thought it may have been the Prime Minister. I'm expecting a call from him.'

'Really?'

'You idiot! Of course not! What do you want?'

'Have you been able to work out a way that I can meet Chris?'

I remembered my terrible faux pas from earlier in the day, and I told her what had happened.

There was a shocked silence from Kim. 'You're kidding,' she said, finally.

'I wish I were.'

'Rosie, that was the last thing I wanted to happen! I wanted to—oh! Never mind. What did he say?'

I thought back carefully to Chris's response. 'He didn't really say anything,' I said. 'All he said was, *She still lives here?*'

'She still lives here?'

'Yep.'

'I mean, was it a hopeful *She still lives here,* or a shocked *She still lives here* as if I've never done anything with my life, or was it—'

'I'm going to bed.'

Hanging up, I lay my head on the pillow and took a deep breath. *I don't feel tired. Maybe I'll read for a while.* The next thing I knew, I was awake again. I blinked, confused about where I was. *That's right. The Lighthouse Inn.* The room lay in darkness. The tree at the window was moving slightly in the wind. A branch clawed at the glass. I glanced at the clock.

12.10am.

Voices came from the hallway.

What's going on out there?

I eased my door open a crack and peered out. There was nothing further up the hall, but now I recognised one of the voices: Cameron Dark.

I went to the top of the stairs and peered down. Cameron was down in the hall, deep in conversation with Dorothy.

'—can't do anything for you,' he was saying.

'But I came all this way to see you,' she hissed.

'Then you've wasted your time!'

I crept back to my room. Climbing into bed, I turned out the light and lay there wondering about what I'd just seen. Was an illicit rendezvous going on between Cameron and Dorothy? How was that possible? They'd barely spoken. Was she as starstruck as Charlotte? Cameron and Katy didn't seem close. Maybe this went on all the time.

Sleep came. Then—

1:56am

I lay in the darkness with no idea of what had woken me. Listening hard, all I could hear was the distant sound of the wind. A piece of metal was clanging somewhere.

Why am I awake?

Cracking my door open, I peered into the hallway and heard the shuffle of feet on the stairs. *What's going on down there?* Heading to the top of the stairs, I was just in time to see a shape disappearing from sight.

That was Katy Dark!

What was she doing? I listened hard. Nothing. Then there was the sound of a door opening. *Is she going outside?* The door clicked shut again. I shivered. *It's freezing out here.* Scurrying back to bed, I allowed the dark to settle around me. Minutes passed. It was after two now. The wind sang and moaned in the night.

How strange, I thought. *Where was Katy Dark going...*

Darkness. A dream about singing cupcakes. I was speaking to Todd. *You can't do it all alone. You need help.* A voice came from a great distance. A man was talking. Todd? No, not Todd. And he wasn't talking to me.

'...wouldn't go out this early alone,' the voice was saying. 'She certainly wouldn't leave Garry.'

Blinking, I opened my eyes. Early morning light cast a grey glow across the room. It took a moment for everything to come back: the inn, the dinner party, Katy Dark. The voice I could hear belonged to Cameron Dark.

Throwing on a dressing gown, I cautiously went to my door and peered out. Cameron was in the hallway speaking to Sheila.

'Well, the front door is shut,' Sheila was saying. 'Although it is unlocked.'

'But she wouldn't go out without Garry,' Cameron insisted. 'She takes him everywhere.'

Cindy leaned out her doorway. 'What's happening?'

'I was heading out for a walk when I noticed Katy's door ajar,' Cameron said. 'This was on her bed.'

We gathered around him as he held up the note. It was crudely written as if scrawled by someone in a rage. It read:

You deserve to die. I will get you.

'How horrible,' I said, thinking. 'I saw Katy around two o'clock. She was going outside.'

'At two in the morning?' Cameron said. 'Then she may not have come back. We need to find her. Ring the police. Organise a search.'

At that moment, Chadek came up the stairs. 'I have searched the house and the garden.' His hair was unruly, and he was unshaved. Obviously, he had been roused by Cameron and sent to find the missing woman. 'Mrs Dark is not there.'

'Then we need to get the police!'

Chadek shook his head. 'I doubt they will come,' he said, pronouncing his I as *ee*. 'They will think she has just gone out for a walk.'

'The rest of us can search,' I suggested. 'She's probably fine. There may be no connection between her disappearance and the note.'

People came out of their rooms.

Charlotte appeared, looking the worse for wear. Then Colin and Chris. While they were told what had happened, I went away to get dressed and was back out again in minutes.

By then, the place was a hive of activity, and people seemed to be scurrying about, getting nowhere. In the midst of it, Cameron made calls on his phone, and a dazed Sheila Birdwhistle roamed from room to room as if Katy might magically appear from a crack in the wall.

Colin passed by me and sighed. 'Much ado about nothing,' he murmured.

'Has she done this sort of thing before?'

'Variations on a theme. You really can't blame her. She's monitored twenty-four-seven. Must be an absolute joy to wander about freely.'

Threatening letters weren't left on her pillow every day, though, I thought. *Maybe something has happened to her.*

I headed outside. A fog had come in overnight, wrapping the coast in a woollen shawl. It was impossible to see either Cape Carson or West beach. Walking through it was like wandering through a dream. The only sound breaking the eerie silence was the sloshing of the waves against the shore. Then I heard Cameron calling Katy's name. Then another voice—Cindy—joined in. And someone else. Another man.

Fog reduced visibility to a few feet. It took me by surprise when a white shape loomed before me. I'd reached the lighthouse. The structure stood like some ancient monolith. My gaze travelled up and down its length, and I glimpsed the sky. The high cloud was being scorched orange by the early light of day.

Cameron was probably worried about nothing. Or was he? My mind returned to the note. It *was* ominous. And Katy had left in the middle of the night. It was a long time to be out in a town she barely knew.

Rounding the lighthouse, I spotted a slender black rectangle cut into its side: the lighthouse door was cracked open.

What the—?

Without thinking, I strode over and gave it a shove. *She's gone up to look at the view.* But as I started up the stairs, a jangle of concern stirred in the pit of my stomach. I'd walked to the lighthouse hundreds of times and never seen the door open. The place was operated by the local Historical Society. They wouldn't leave it unlocked. I reached the top. It was freezing in the lighthouse, and I could see why. The door leading to the gallery was open.

My feet clanged on the metal platform as I stepped out. It was like floating among the clouds. The fog pressed in on all sides as I rounded the gantry. I was halfway around, at the point where I would have been facing the sea, when I saw the feet. Then the legs. A few seconds later, I saw Katy Dark sitting on the metal gantry, her back against the wall of the lantern room. She was staring out at the endless, moving fog.

'Katy?' I hissed. 'Are you okay?'

She didn't answer because she couldn't. A knife lay jammed in her chest. The blood from the wound ran down her front and gathered in a pool by her side. It was from this that Katy Dark, with her dying breath, had scrawled a last message to identify her killer:

C

8

'I need to speak to each of you,' Todd said. 'One at a time. I'll ask that you not leave the hotel, and certainly not the area.'

Everyone was sitting around the Lighthouse Inn's dining room. The morning fog had lifted by then, and it was possible to see the town and most of the coast. I'd contacted the police before breaking the news to Cameron and the others.

Todd, his offsider, Constable Jim Turner, and several other constables had arrived to find Chadek holding Cameron back as he tried to enter the lighthouse.

'You must not go up,' the bodyguard had said. 'The police need to examine the crime scene.'

'Chadek's right,' I added. 'I'm sorry.'

Cameron Dark's grey eyes had filled with tears. 'But it's my wife,' he said, dazed. 'Katy needs me...'

That's when the police arrived.

I gazed around the assembled group: Cindy, Chris, Colin, Chadek, Charlotte, and Cameron. *The Six Cees.* It had all seemed funny the night before. Now there was a good chance that one of them had murdered Katy Dark. Unfortunately, no one had obliged us by confessing to the crime. They all looked stunned. All except for Cameron, who had collapsed into a pattern of weepy tears and a weary shaking of his head.

'How could this have happened?' Cindy asked. 'Why was Katy at the lighthouse?'

'She had no reason to go there,' Cameron muttered, turning to me. 'And you saw her leave?'

'It was just before two o'clock,' I said. 'I heard a noise and got out of bed. I saw Katy heading downstairs and then outside.'

Cameron looked shellshocked. 'But where was she going?'

'I have no idea.'

'Cameron,' Todd said. 'It's early in our investigation. We won't have all the answers until we've spoken to everyone involved. That's why I'm asking you and everyone else to stay here.'

A knock came from the door, and a constable entered with Kim.

'Rosie?' Kim said.

'Kim?'

My chest swelled with relief. Despite seeing deceased people before, Katy's dead body had shocked me to the core. Seeing Kim's friendly face brought me back to reality.

'This is Kim,' I said to the constable. 'My...photographer.'

Todd said nothing, but I saw his chin tighten. He knew Kim was there to give me moral support—and maybe something more. Kim and I had a track record of amateur sleuthing, which Todd thought of as *sticking your nose in*. It wasn't something he approved of, despite our previous success.

I saw Kim's eyes sweep the room before settling on Chris. He inclined his head and she gave him the tiniest of nods. Kim's face was unreadable, although this was clearly not how she had envisioned her reunion with Chris.

Todd asked Kim and I to go out to reception and wait for him. We went to the front desk with Trixie trailing us. It was strangely quiet out here. There were police roaming around the gardens.

A few were assembled at the base of the lighthouse. It looked like a forensics van had arrived. They would probably finger-print the area and take photos before removing Katy's body.

Kim gave me a hug. 'I heard what happened,' she said. 'I came as soon as I could.'

'It's good seeing you.'

'You found her body?'

'It was a horrible shock. I thought we'd find Katy wandering along the beach somewhere. She mustn't have returned after I saw her leave.' I glanced back towards the dining room. 'We'll speak to the others as soon as Todd finishes with them. I hope you're okay to help.'

'Are you kidding? You know how much I love this stuff. Not the actual murder,' she hastened to add. 'But finding the killer!'

'It could be dangerous.'

'How bad can it be?'

'Well, Katy Dark got stabbed in the chest.'

'Hmm.' Kim's face dropped. 'That's pretty bad.'

The dining-room door opened, and Todd appeared with Cameron. Todd told the actor to wait in the library while he spoke to us.

'All right,' Todd said in a low voice as soon as Cameron had disappeared from sight. 'Can I trust both of you to keep out of the way?'

'Of course,' we said in unison.

Todd groaned. 'No, seriously,' he said. 'I've got a killer to find.'

'I know,' I said. 'But aren't two heads better than one? And three must be fantastic. And, Todd, haven't I told you since you arrived in this town that everyone in Cape Carson helps each other?'

'You've said that a lot. So can you explain why it is that I had to arrest Thelma Marshall for trying to steal all the flour from Casey's Supermarket?'

I processed this. 'When you say *all* the flour....'

'Forty kilos of it. Thelma was trying to smuggle it out in the shopping cart of her mobility scooter. She did it to stop other people making cupcakes.'

'I did say the Cupcake Festival brings out the best and the worst in people.'

'You'll get no argument from me.'

Kim added. 'And Thelma's always taking things,' she said. 'We've caught her stealing library books at least half a dozen times. I don't know why. They're free to borrow!'

'There is something I should ask you,' I said to Todd. 'Did you see what Katy had written beside her body?'

'The letter C?'

'It looks like Katy was trying to write her killer's name.'

Kim spoke up. 'That hardly narrows it down.'

'Unfortunately, you're right,' I said.

'Ladies.' Todd held up a hand. 'You need to leave this to us.'

I continued on unabated. 'There are six people here whose name starts with C: Cameron, Chris, Cindy, Colin, Charlotte, and Chadek. I can do half the interviews, and you can do the other—'

Todd shook his head.

'Kim and I can be helpful,' I said, stubbornly.

Trixie whined.

'Maybe,' Todd said. 'But this is police business.'

Telling us again to stay out of his way, Todd headed to the library and closed the door behind him.

'Okay,' I said. 'We've got a crime to solve.'

'You're going to ignore Todd?' Kim said.

'He said to stay out of his way. We'll do that—and hopefully, find the killer at the same time. Besides, I'm a member of the press and have a right to make inquiries. And, Kim, you're my trusty…photographer.' I glanced at the phone in her hand. 'We've really got to get you a real camera.'

She peered down at the phone. 'Don't bother,' she said. 'Then I'd need to learn how to use it.'

I went on to tell Kim everything that had happened from the time I arrived at the Lighthouse Inn.

'The killer can't be Chris,' Kim said at the end.

'Kim, I know you had a relationship with him a million years ago, but he might have changed.'

'That's possible,' Kim grudgingly agreed. 'But what motive would he have for killing Katy?'

'I have no idea. Anyway, let's get started.'

'Sheila?'

I nodded. 'Sheila.'

Ten minutes later, we were in the study sitting opposite the landlady. I felt sorry for her. The woman looked like she'd aged twenty years overnight. This was obviously a disaster in so many ways. The Lighthouse Inn would forever be linked to the murder of Katy Dark. And running an establishment where people got killed was not the sort of reputation an inn owner wanted for their business. Trixie placed her head on the woman's knee and Sheila absently patted her.

'Nothing like this has ever happened before,' she said. 'Apart from old Mister Richie dying, but that wasn't murder. He fell off the roof while hanging Christmas decorations in 1985. I suppose you could also include Sandra with her heart attack except—'

'Sheila,' I interrupted. 'The Historical Society has a key to the lighthouse, but Todd told me it's accounted for. What about the one you keep here?'

The woman paled. 'That was the first thing the officer checked,' she said. 'The one beside the reception desk is gone. It was there yesterday, and today it's not. It's been stolen!'

I nodded.

It had been there yesterday. Everyone had probably noticed it when they booked in. Which meant that any of the guests could have stolen it.

'It's never gone missing before,' Sheila said. 'Although, a few years back, it fell off and got swept up by accident by that girl Martha who was working here. She was no good though, so we got rid of her—'

'Sheila.' Trying to keep her focused was like trying to herd kittens. 'When was the last time you saw it on display?'

She thought for a long moment. 'It was late in the evening,' she said. 'I dusted around all the pieces. Having celebrity guests, I suddenly realised they might leave negative reviews of the inn if they noticed any dust. So I cleaned.'

'Do you have security cameras?' Kim asked.

'No. We've never needed them before.'

I spoke. 'So you stay here in the inn?'

'I've got a room out the back.'

'And Dorothy and Jason?'

'Jason lives in Barkly.' That was a small town north of Cape Carson. 'He leaves straight after dinner. Dorothy lives in the bungalow out the back.'

'And the key was still there when Jason left?' I asked.

'I think so,' she said. 'Yes, I'm sure it was. I remember taking a last look around just before I went to bed. Jason was gone by then. Dorothy was waiting for the guests to finish. I distinctly recall looking around at the display pieces and thinking they all looked better.'

'But Jason could have returned.'

Sheila shook her head firmly. 'His keys unlock the back door leading into the kitchen,' she said. 'But you noticed the door from the dining room? I lock it every night. Jason's keys gets him as far as the dining room, but no further.'

So that rules Jason out.

'I recently fired a staff member for stealing,' Sheila said. 'It's not like the old days when you could trust people—'

'Does Dorothy have a key?' I asked.

'Yes. To the whole building.'

'And the front door was locked last night?' Kim asked.

'I always shut the place up tightly every night. We had a drunk burst in late one night a few years back. Well, he wasn't really a drunk. More of a—'

'Cameron mentioned a threatening note,' I said. 'One that arrived yesterday. Can you tell us about it?'

'Well, we found one on the counter after everyone came back from the lighthouse.'

'So that was around six o'clock?'

Sheila thought. 'Yes.'

'Any thoughts about who could have left it there?'

'It could have been anyone,' Sheila said, shrugging. 'The front door is open during the day, so anyone walking by could have dropped it on the counter.'

'And you gave the letter to Katy?'

'To Cindy. That girl who works for her.' She stopped. 'Worked for her.'

'And another one turned up today?'

'Mister Dark found it on Katy's bed. I suppose someone could have come in the front door and gone up the stairs—'

Kim cut in. 'So the front door was unlocked?'

'Katy must have left it open when she went out.' Sheila shook her head. 'First time we've ever had something like this happen.'

'Can you think of anything else?' Kim asked. 'Something else unusual that's happened?'

Sheila looked sideways. 'Maybe,' she said. 'I mean, I told that nice policeman what I found out there. It could be something, or nothing or—'

'What was it?' I asked.

'A crowbar.'

'A crowbar?'

'Just a tiny one,' Sheila said. 'Not much bigger than your hand.'

Kim and I exchanged glances.

'Can you show us?' I asked.

We followed Sheila outside. The barbeque behind the inn was old: square, brick, and unattractive. It looked rarely used, although the ashes had been recently disturbed.

'I noticed it this morning,' Sheila said. 'When I came out here looking for Katy, I happened to glance down into the fireplace and saw something in there. It stood out because we haven't had a barbeque for ages.'

'And you gave it to the police?' I said.

Sheila said she had. We asked her a few more questions, but she had nothing else to share. The landlady headed inside, leaving me, Trixie and Kim to follow slowly into the building.

'What do you think?' I asked Kim.

'Only that Sheila seems to have narrowed the list of suspects to the hotel guests. With the front door locked and dining room secured, only one of them could have taken the key.'

'Or Dorothy or Sheila.' I stopped. 'They both have keys to the whole building. Otherwise, you're right. It's down to the guests which means it may have been Katy. The real question, though, is what made Katy go to the lighthouse.'

We returned to the study. 'What do you think of Katy and Cameron's relationship?' she asked.

'They're about as happy together as two unhappy people can be,' I said. 'Mind you, I saw them together for less than twenty-four hours, but they seemed to have no interest in each other. It doesn't surprise me. I've met a lot of celebrity couples, and many of them live apart, which explains why their marriages don't last.'

'Did you see anything to make you think he wanted her dead?'

'Nothing. Except...'

'What?'

'There's the Horizon Ring,' I said. Kim didn't know about it, so I quickly explained the value and history of the ring. 'I'm assuming it's still in Katy's safe.'

'Todd will check on that. If it's gone...'

'Then it's a good motive for murder. Meanwhile, we need to speak to Cameron Dark. He's the obvious suspect. Nine times out of ten, husbands kill their wives.'

I thought back to seeing Cameron and Katy together. They hadn't been close. That was obvious.

But why would Cameron Dark murder his wife?

9

'So why should I speak to you?' Cameron Dark asked.

The tears had vanished from Cameron's face by the time he joined us in the study. In the morning chaos, he'd found time to shower and change. He now wore Levi jeans, a black t-shirt, and a Saint Laurent jacket. Inhaling, I recognised his cologne as Giorgio Armani.

He's recovering well, I thought. *Considering his wife has only been dead a few hours.*

'Because you need to get ahead of the story,' I said. 'A lot will be said about Katy's death in the coming weeks. I can share your side. Besides,' I said, lowering my voice, 'at least I knew you and Katy.'

I hadn't known them well—hardly at all, really—but I hoped this would portray me as more sympathetic than the jackals that had gathered outside.

At least half a dozen journalists were circling like vultures near the gate. They'd obviously flown out here to get the scoop on Katy's death.

Cameron gazed into space. 'I suppose that's true. At least you saw us in those last hours together.'

'Cameron,' I said, forging ahead. 'I hope you don't mind me saying this, but you and Katy didn't seem particularly...'

'Close?' Cameron Dark gave a bitter laugh. 'We weren't. The love was long gone. But that doesn't mean I killed her.'

'Can I ask your whereabouts after the party?'

Cameron didn't speak.

Kim spoke up. 'Silence won't help,' she said. 'Not at a time like this.'

'I suppose it'll eventually come out,' Cameron said. 'I was with Cindy.'

'Cindy Hillspring?' I said.

'We've been in a relationship if you must know. My wife and I have had an understanding for some time,' Cameron said, shooting me a look. 'You've been in the business. You know what I mean.'

I knew what he meant, although it was rarely mentioned out loud. Many people in the entertainment industry seemed happily married, but it was a different story behind closed doors. They were often carrying on a string of affairs—with or without their partner's knowledge.

'It happens,' I said.

'Katy's career has been exploding,' Cameron said. 'While

my own career has somewhat waned. Not that I've been too worried by that. Acting is a tough business, and I've done well, all things considered. I was happy to support Katy. She was single-minded. You have to grab the opportunities when they happen. There's precious few.' He paused. 'That means her focus was elsewhere. Not on me. Or us. Maybe it's inevitable that something should eventuate between Cindy and me.'

'How long has the relationship been going on?' Kim asked.

Cameron shrugged. 'Nine months.'

'And Katy knew about it?'

'We didn't discuss it openly if that's what you're asking. However, I'm sure Katy knew. There was a business meeting that Cindy had to attend last month, and I went with her. Katy knew and didn't object.'

Don't ask, I thought. *And don't tell.*

'Did anyone else know about the affair?' I asked.

'Affair is such a tawdry word.'

'All right. Did anyone else know about your relationship?'

'I don't think so, but it's possible. And it wasn't just me that sought comfort elsewhere.'

There was a momentary silence. Then Kim spoke up. 'You're saying Katy also had...another relationship?' she said. 'With whom?'

'I'm not sure,' Cameron said, looking away. 'Perhaps you could ask Chris.'

Although I'm sure Cameron missed it, I saw the flash of disappointment in Kim's eyes. It was like watching a fire get doused with water. I reminded myself to give her a big hug later.

'You're saying Katy was having a relationship with Chris Dawson?' I said.

'You'd have to ask him.'

Kim swallowed. 'Can you tell us your movements after the dinner party?'

He frowned in thought. 'The dinner continued until about midnight when I headed up to my room. I was there for about half an hour before going to Cindy's room for the night. Awoke in the middle of the night—maybe around half-past two—and posted pictures to social media. They were shots I'd taken from the lighthouse. You can check if you want. They have a timestamp showing when I uploaded them.

'Around six-thirty, I awoke and was returning to my room when I noticed Katy's door ajar. Garry was in there alone, and the note was on the bed.'

'I suppose Cindy can vouch for this.'

'Yes.'

'And the rest of the night?'

'Like most other people,' he said, 'I was asleep.'

'And you raised the alarm this morning?' Kim asked.

Cameron nodded. 'Everyone was up within minutes,' he

said. 'First, I searched the building, and then the grounds around the property. It was foggy and hard to see. I had no idea what had happened to Katy, but I hoped she'd be safe. I didn't think...' He spoke with sudden anguish. 'I loved Katy. You have to understand that. And she loved me. Our little dalliances meant nothing. What I don't understand is why she was at the lighthouse. Why there?'

I didn't have an answer for that.

My mind returned to the lighthouse. Her motionless body. The knife. The pool of blood. The letter *C* painted with her right index finger.

'Does the letter *C* have any particular meaning to you?' I asked.

'The policeman asked that as well. He said...' Cameron swallowed hard. 'He said Katy wrote it with her dying breath. Why would she do that? To identify her killer?'

That was the obvious reason. Except it didn't do that. It didn't achieve anything. There were six people at the Lighthouse Inn whose names started with C. It could be any of them. Worse, it could be someone outside our group. Another person whose name started with C.

Or, worst-case scenario, it could mean nothing at all. Just a misfiring neuron in Katy's brain as she lay dying.

Cameron Dark bit his lip. 'There's that woman Charlotte,' he said. 'Could she have killed Katy?'

Charlotte had struck me as slightly odd, except she had no reason to kill Katy. She'd entered the competition so she could meet her. And she hadn't shown the slightest animosity towards the movie star. 'Katy could have gone to the lighthouse to look at the view,' I said. 'I suppose Charlotte could have followed her.'

'Had Katy ever met Charlotte before?' Kim asked.

'Not as far as I know.' Cameron rubbed his face. 'I'm sorry. I'm exhausted, and I've already gone through all this with that police officer.'

I thanked him for his time, and he got up to leave.

'Cameron,' I said. 'Just one thing.'

'Yes?'

'Last night, I saw you speaking to Dorothy. It was just after midnight.'

He shook his head. 'It was nothing. She's an autograph hunter. It was late, and I was in no mood to be corralled.'

I nodded, thinking of the way she'd been speaking to him.

What did Dorothy say? *But I came all this way to see you. What did she mean?*

'Is that all?' Cameron asked.

'Sure,' I said, although I didn't believe him.

Something was fishy here. The question was—*what?*

10

'Thanks for speaking with us,' I said.

Charlotte Bannister sat back in her chair.

She looked remarkably composed, considering this was a murder investigation. Charlotte patted Trixie before reaching into her bag and pulling out a bunch of knitting. It looked like a half-completed scarf.

'I'm very happy to help,' she said. 'It's an awful thing that's happened. Everyone's terribly upset.'

'And you?'

'Oh yes,' Charlotte said as her fingers started wrapping wool around the needles. 'I hope you don't mind me knitting. It always settles my nerves.'

'So you liked Katy Dark as an actress?' Kim ventured.

'She was wonderful in all her movies.'

'Winning the contest was a lucky break,' I said. 'Do you enter many contests?'

'A few. I have my own money through an inheritance from

my mother. I own my own home. It's all paid off. Entering contests is a hobby. I've won a lot of things over the years. Weekends away. Books. Food hampers. All kinds of things.'

'Where do you live?' I asked.

'Bombatta.'

I knew the place. Located about fifty kilometres north of Cape Carson, it was so tiny the place barely warranted a dot on the map.

'It's quiet out there,' I said.

The knitting needles clicked. 'There are busier places.'

'What time did you arrive here yesterday?'

'Around five o'clock, I think.'

'You didn't like your room?'

Charlotte's eyes flickered up at me. 'I wanted a view,' she said. 'That wasn't unreasonable.'

'You're lucky that Chris was prepared to swap with you.'

'He was happy to do that, and I appreciated it.'

'You said something about your allocated room.' I thought hard. 'What was it? Oh, yes. *It's not what I needed.* What did you mean by that?'

'Did I say that? I don't recall it.'

'What did you mean?'

'I obviously misspoke.' She gave a tiny shoulder shrug. 'It means nothing.'

Kim cut in. 'What time did you go to bed?'

'Sometime after eleven.' Charlotte lowered her knitting and gave a small laugh. 'I actually fell asleep at the dinner table. I don't know if anyone noticed; they were all so sozzled. Alcohol always makes me sleepy. A few of the others were still partying on, but I'd had enough.'

'Did you hear anything during the night?' I asked.

Charlotte frowned. 'Like I told the police officer,' she said. 'There was a thud around half-past two as if something was dropped.'

'Do you know where the sound came from?' Kim asked.

'Katy's room—I think. It's hard to say.'

I spoke up. 'You're probably aware that Katy received some threatening letters in the weeks leading up to her death?'

'Yes. Cameron mentioned one yesterday. And there was the one on her bed this morning.'

'Do you know anything about that?'

'Why would I?' Charlotte put down her knitting. 'Look, the policeman asked me the same silly questions. So let me ask you this: why would I kill Katy? I *loved* Katy. She was a talented actress, and meeting her was a thrill.'

'So you don't know anything about the letters?'

'No.' Charlotte smirked. 'Maybe Katy went to meet someone at the lighthouse. A lover, maybe.'

'You have someone in mind?' I asked.

The needles started clattering again. 'I saw that man, Chris

Dawson, and Katy together in the upstairs hallway just before dinner. They looked *very* friendly.'

It seemed everyone knew about them.

'How friendly?' Kim asked, her voice even.

'I don't know,' she said. 'You'll have to ask him that.'

We had no more questions for Charlotte. After she left, I eased the door shut and turned to Kim. 'It really seems like—'

'Chris and Katy were in a relationship,' she said. 'And Cameron was playing around with Cindy.'

'So much for happy couples.'

Kim shrugged. 'That's show business.'

There was an underlying sadness to the comment and I knew why. 'I'm sorry,' I said sympathetically. 'I know you were hoping that something would happen with Chris.'

'I was silly,' Kim said, sighing. 'That summer was a long time ago. He's had a life since then. Me too. And he was travelling with one of the country's most famous actresses. If it came between her and me...'

She looked ready to burst into tears, and I took her hand. 'Cheer up, Kim,' I said. 'Don't forget—we're Cape Carson's greatest detectives.'

'You might be. I'm just a librarian.'

'There's no such thing as *just* a librarian.'

Kim sniffed. 'Well,' she assented. 'That's true. Librarians are the unsung champions of the book world.'

'So true,' I said. 'Come on. The game's afoot, and I need you. I can't do this alone.'

Squeezing my hand, Kim stood. 'Okay, Holmes,' she said. 'But that line about the game being afoot never made any sense to me.'

'Me neither.'

A few minutes later, we had convinced Cindy that it was in her best interest to speak with us, and she had joined us in the study. It made sense to interview her next. Cindy was Cameron's alibi. If Cindy didn't back him up, then his story meant nothing.

Despite only the passage of a few hours, Cindy looked even smaller than before. The tragedy of Katy's death had probably shaken her in more ways than one. As well as her employer being dead, it meant her meal ticket had also come to an end.

Trixie placed her head on Cindy's knee and the publicist stroked her back.

I got straight to business. 'Can you describe your movements after the dinner party?'

'There's not much to tell. I went to bed.'

'Around eleven-thirty?'

She nodded.

'Is it true you've been having a relationship with Cameron Dark?' I asked.

Cindy's face reddened under her straw-coloured hair. 'Who

told you that?'

'Cameron.'

Her voice rose an octave. 'It's true,' she said defensively. 'It doesn't mean anything. It was just a bit of fun.'

'Did Cameron go to your room last night?' Kim asked.

'Yes. At about twelve-thirty.'

'And were you awake after that?'

Cindy nodded. 'As it happens, I was,' she said. 'I woke up when Cameron got us water at about two o'clock. I remember because he asked me what time it was. I couldn't find my phone, but I distinctly remember looking at the clock. We lay awake for about half an hour before going off to sleep.'

'Did Cameron do anything on social media?' I asked carefully.

'Oh, yes,' Cindy said, remembering. 'He put some pictures online before we drifted off to sleep. I often have problems sleeping. Sometimes I even take a Stilnox. Not last night, though. Once I was out, I was out like a light. It had been a big day. Anyway, next thing I knew, it was early morning, and Cameron was still with me. I told him to go back to his room.'

'Cameron told us you couldn't find your phone.'

'It had slipped under the bed. That's all.'

I quickly checked Cameron's account. The images had been posted around two-thirty.

Kim asked Cindy about her job. 'You're Katy's manager?'

'No. I'm her publicist. Cameron has been managing Katy since she got rid of Colin.'

'Why was he replaced?'

'Although Colin was able to get Katy acting roles, he wasn't good with the financial side. Actually, he was hopeless, by the sound of it. There's money all over the place in different accounts and different investments. It'll take years to sort out.'

'Was Colin unhappy about being replaced?' I asked.

Cindy sighed. 'Well, he wasn't overjoyed. He felt betrayed that Katy had gotten rid of him.'

'So, how did he end up here?'

'When Colin found out that Katy was coming to Cape Carson for the weekend, he virtually forced her to invite him. And Katy has always found it hard—' She stopped. 'I mean, she always found it hard to say no.'

'Why did he want to be here?' Kim asked.

'Why do you think? To get his old job back—but that would never happen. Despite having a soft spot for Colin, Katy was done with him. Her career was taking off, and she wasn't looking back. It wasn't anything personal against Colin. She'd moved on. That's all.'

We asked Cindy a few more questions, including if she could shed light on the letter C that Katy had written with her own blood. Cindy had no idea. The interview over, she made it as far as the door before stopping.

'I don't know who killed Katy,' she said. 'But I will say one thing. Cameron and I had nothing to do with it. We're not in love—our relationship isn't like that—and we had nothing to gain from Katy's death. She was worth more alive to us than dead!'

11

'Tell us about your relationship with Katy Dark,' I said.

Chris Dawson shrugged. 'What do you want to know?'

It had been a long morning, and it wasn't over yet. We'd already interviewed three people from the household—Sheila, Cameron, and Cindy—and we still had Chris, Colin, and Chadek to go. And all that talking would only get us to a starting point. A place where we could begin to grasp what had happened to Katy.

Kim seemed calm, although she didn't have me fooled. This would be a challenging interview. Behind that serene exterior, I knew she was churning with emotion.

'We understand you were in a relationship with her,' she said. 'Something beyond professional.'

'Kim,' he said. 'I don't know what this is about. If you're inferring that I was having an affair with Katy—'

'We know you were,' I interrupted. 'Chris, we're just trying to do what's right. Katy's gone, and we need to put all the pieces together to understand who's responsible.'

The writer gazed at us silently. 'All right,' he said. 'It's true. We were having an affair.'

'How did that come about?'

'As you know, I make my living as a ghostwriter. Sometimes my name appears on the cover; sometimes, it doesn't. I did that biography last year of Phil Malone, the footballer. The year before that, I cowrote Stan Green's book. He was the soldier who lost both legs in Afghanistan.' Chris stopped. 'I was excited to be contracted to Katy Dark. I'd admired her as an actress, and I thought it would be a big step in my career. I'd only been working with her for a week when the affair began.'

'That's fast work,' Kim commented.

Chris met her eye. 'I suppose it was,' he said. 'Katy made it happen. I can't say I fought it, although I did question its morality. When I mentioned her husband, Katy just laughed and said they both did this kind of thing all the time.'

'Did Cameron know about your relationship?'

'I don't know. Katy said he didn't, but I wasn't so sure. Sometimes I felt that Cameron knew and wasn't saying.' He paused. 'Besides, he's been in a fling with Cindy.'

Kim and I exchanged glances. It seemed that nothing was secret in their group.

'Really?' I said.

'I've seen Cameron leaving Cindy's room early in the morning.' Chris smiled wryly. 'Cameron can hardly complain about Katy and me when he's been….' His voice trailed away, and he looked lost. 'My goodness. Katy's gone. I can hardly believe it.'

'I'm sorry,' Kim said quietly.

Chris nodded. 'Me too.' He looked up at Kim. 'I can hardly believe I'm seeing you again after all these years. It's like a dream.'

'For me too,' Kim said. 'I wondered about you over the years. What had happened to you.'

'Life,' Chris said, shrugging. 'Grew up. Got older. Married. Divorced. And you?'

'The same.'

Their gaze lingered.

This was all very heartwarming, but a woman had been murdered, and we were trying to find her killer. 'Can you tell us your movements last night?' I asked. 'After dinner?'

He stirred. 'Well,' he said. 'The dinner party broke up around midnight. Katy and I had both already decided that spending the night together here at the inn was too risky. Charlotte was an outsider and—no offense—you're a journalist. We didn't want our story getting out.'

'So you didn't see Katy after you went to bed?'

'No.'

'Did you hear anything unusual?'

Chris paused. 'You know, now that you mention it, there

was something,' he said. 'I remember waking at some point. There was a thud as if something hit the floor.'

'Any idea what time that was?'

'Maybe after two. I dimly remember glancing at the clock and seeing two-something.'

Kim spoke up. 'Can you think of any reason why Katy would leave the building in the middle of the night?'

'No.'

I rubbed my chin. 'Sergeant Parker has already mentioned about the letter *C* next to Katy's body?'

'Yes,' Chris said, swallowing. 'The officer did tell me. I don't know what that means. Other than it could refer to that woman Charlotte. She's downright odd. Maybe Katy was trying to tell us that Charlotte attacked her.'

'In what way is she odd?'

'Considering she's supposed to be a fan of Katy's, she barely spoke to her. Maybe she was starstruck, but she seemed more interested in Cameron than Katy.'

Kim spoke up. 'Do you think it's possible that Cameron had anything to do with Katy's death?'

'The same idea's crossed my mind,' Chris said. 'He is the obvious suspect, after all. The husband's usually guilty, but it seems unlikely in this case. Despite how odd it may sound, Cameron and Katy had a happy marriage. They never argued, and he seemed happy to ride on Katy's wave of success.'

'There is the Horizon Ring,' I pointed out. 'That's worth a lot of money.'

'Except Cameron won't inherit it. Katy mentioned once that she'd already made out her will. The ring will go to a favourite cousin.'

'I see.'

'Is there anything else you can add?' Kim asked, but the writer shook his head.

'Thanks for talking with us,' I said.

Chris's eyes settled on Kim. 'It's nice to see you again,' he said. 'Maybe we can have a chat over coffee. A talk about something other than Katy's death.'

'That would be nice.'

He left, the door clicking quietly shut behind him.

'That must have been hard,' I said.

'Not so hard,' Kim said. 'It's been a long time. He's still the same, though. Different, but the same. Older. More handsome. The guy I spent that summer with was skinny and kind of dorky. He's grown into himself.'

I nodded. 'He's confirmed a few things, at least. He and Katy were in a relationship. And he knew about Cameron and Cindy.' I paused. 'And Cameron doesn't stand to inherit the ring.'

'Which makes it even less likely that he killed her,' Kim said. 'And Chris also heard that bump in the night.'

'The one that Charlotte mentioned? I wonder what it was.'

Leaving Kim in the study, I found Colin in the dining room. Agreeing to come and talk to us, he was soon settling into the seat opposite.

'I'm always happy to meet with beautiful women,' he said.

'Well,' Kim said. 'No faulting your taste.'

Colin continued. 'Plus, it's important that the truth be told. The media can do that. I'd rather set the record straight before the rumours fly.'

'Can you account for your movements last night after the party?' I asked.

'Absolutely. I went to bed and didn't stir again until this morning when Cameron raised the alarm.'

'Did you hear anything during the night?'

'Such as?'

'Any odd sounds? Anything out of the ordinary?'

Colin laughed. 'I'm not sure what constitutes an odd sound in this quiet part of the world,' he said. 'Maybe the hooting of an owl. No, there was nothing. Just the sound of the wind. I didn't hear Katy leave the building or anything concerning her death.'

'You don't seem very upset,' Kim said, carefully.

'Katy was the actor,' he said. 'I'm not. I'm her ex-manager, and she wasn't always easy to get along with. Mind you, I am sorry she's dead. She had talent but no idea of loyalty.' He held up a hand. 'And before you ask, she did not treat me well. The first time I saw her, she was demonstrating washing powder in a supermarket in Sandringham. I thought she had potential. A face that people would pay to see. So I spent years getting her parts that eventually led to her becoming the lead of the movie *Tokyo Hill*. Her name exploded, and producers came begging to her door.' He paused. 'And you know what she did? She replaced me with her husband who couldn't manage a lemonade stand, let alone an acting career.'

'Katy's career seemed to be on the rise,' I said. 'If Cameron had no managing abilities—'

'Katy also got Cindy onboard. Cindy had worked for Hawke and Sota Management. They're an internationally renowned publicity agency. I don't blame Cindy. She had the connections to take Katy to the next level.'

'But you came here this weekend.'

'I was invited. Katy clearly had no idea how much she'd hurt me. I cornered her for a few minutes yesterday. I hoped she'd had a change of mind.'

'And had she?'

'She told me it wasn't personal. It was business. I can understand that.'

I considered this. What Colin was saying didn't quite gel with Cindy's words. What did she say?

He virtually forced her to invite him.

Kim asked him about the letter *C* that Katy had written. His answer was the same as the others: Charlotte. Were they pointing her out because she was a stranger to the group? Or because they thought she was the killer? Charlotte *was* a little strange. Was she strange enough to kill Katy?

Nothing could be gleaned from him, so we thanked Colin, and he left.

I turned to Kim. 'There's something here that doesn't tally.'

'I know what you mean. Cindy said that Colin coerced Katy to invite him, and that's not what Colin said.'

'And there's a big difference between pushing your way onto the invitation list or being invited.'

'There's something else too.' Kim leaned close. 'He has beady eyes.'

'Really? I hadn't noticed.'

'You can never trust someone with beady eyes. Rosie, you remember Mrs Whitmore from the Bowls club? They caught her embezzling money.'

'True. But beady eyes aren't a jailable offence.'

'A shame.'

Soon, we had the next person in the study. Chadek sat back in his chair. He looked more relaxed than ever.

'I'm happy to talk to you,' the bodyguard said. 'In Russia, we don't speak to the media. It can get you in hot water. Here in Australia, it can make you a millionaire. I might end up with my own television show after this.'

'We'll see,' I said. 'Now, we're wondering—'

'—if I heard anything during the night?' Chadek said. 'No. I did not. I also don't know who would have killed Katy.'

'You don't suspect anyone?' Kim asked.

'Katy was a fool. I can say that now. She needed to be more careful, and I told her this a thousand times. She laughed.' He shook his head. 'Well, she's not laughing now.'

'How did you get employed by her?' I asked.

'A Melbourne company: Holden Security.'

'And how did you come to be employed by them?'

Chadek explained that he'd moved to Australia and married a woman in Sydney a few years before. The job ended up lasting longer than his marriage. Since then, he'd worked for several wealthy clients. Mostly CEOs, and a few politicians, before being contracted to work with movie and television stars.

'I would say to Katy, don't go near those fans. Did you know that fan is short for fanatic? I did not know that. I told Katy that anyone could be carrying a gun or a knife. But she ignored me. Very foolish.'

Kim spoke. 'Can you think of any reason why she would have gone to the lighthouse last night?'

The bodyguard thought. 'It could have been to meet a lover,' he said. 'There were many of those, including that man

Chris.'

'So Chris and Katy were having an affair?'

'Yes. And Cindy and Cameron also. These celebrities are always hopping from one bed to another. Katy could have gone to the lighthouse to meet Chris. Check his phone. I have known them to venture out at night.'

'Really?'

'They have secret phones, but not so secret. I notice these things. They would send each other messages like teenagers. It was exciting to them. One morning at a hotel in Cairns they left early to—how do you say it—frolic on the beach? They returned before Cameron, and everyone else was awake. I saw them, though. I warned Katy about venturing out alone. Again, she laughed.'

Finally, I asked Chadek if he knew what the C could mean that Katy wrote with her blood.

'Only that it could be that woman. What is her name? Charlotte? I don't like her. She is too quiet. I prefer the admirers when they are loud. They scream and cry and get excited. Then you know where they are.' He paused. 'You should look at the letters too. The threatening ones.'

'You have them?' Kim asked.

'I take them everywhere, just in case something goes wrong.' Chadek let out a long breath, nodding. 'It is fair to say that something has gone wrong.'

Following Chadek from the study, we encountered Sheila in the hallway who told us that the media storm had truly set in. There were now at least twenty reporters out the front. She'd been able to keep them locked out of the property, but the phone was constantly ringing. I told her the best response was to say the police would be issuing a statement later.

Once we were in Chadek's room, he pulled out a shoebox from under his bed and flipped it open to reveal his collection of Katy's hate mail. It was a strange assortment. A lot were from people who didn't like Katy because of her acting. They were more critical than hateful. Others disliked her effect on younger people. These letters said she was a bad influence on girls.

Then there were the bizarre ones. Someone had sent Katy pages ripped from a bible. A man sent her letters saying he was in love with her and they should get married. Another person blamed her for war in the Middle East.

Chadek scooped up a small pile. 'These are the most recent,' he said. 'They're all from the same person.'

These had the same look of being written by someone with their non-dominant hand as if they were desperate to hide their identity. The anger was palpable, not just in words but the way the pen was pressed down hard on the paper. They were downright hostile, saying Katy should die and she was a tramp, and worse things besides.

I shook my head. 'The price of celebrity.'

'Somebody didn't like Katy,' Kim echoed.

'I read a book about stalking a while back,' Chadek said. 'They develop a fixation with people they see on television or in the media. They fantasize about knowing the person in real life and being friends with them. Then if they feel slighted by the celebrity, their attraction turns to hatred.'

'So these are probably from a man?'

'Maybe.' Chadek picked one up. 'This was the one left at the front desk for Katy.'

Kim and I examined it. Similar in tone to the other hand-written samples, something about it made me pause.

What is it?

'This is a different type of paper,' I said. 'The others are all written on something from a writing pad. This paper is better quality.'

'I saw that too,' Chadek said. 'But I don't know what it means.'

My eyes focused on the words on the page:

I hate everything about you. You deserve to die.

'Wow,' Kim said. 'Short and straight to the point.'

A commotion came from the hallway. We put down the threatening letters and went out to see Todd and Constable Turner heading down to Chris's room. It looked like the cops had been searching it. I leaned over Todd's shoulder. The doors of Chris's wardrobe were open, and his suitcase had been upended. But it was what had been lying under the pillow that brought us all to a halt.

I stared. 'Is that—'

'It is,' Todd said.

Lying on the bed was the Horizon Ring.

12

'I don't believe it,' Kim said. 'I can't believe it!'

It was late afternoon, and we were sitting at Sandy's Diner. After Chris's arrest, the remainder of Katy's entourage had been allowed to leave the inn. Finding the ring in Chris's room had just been the beginning. The police had conducted a further search and discovered a burner phone matching one found on Katy. These were the secret phones the pair had used to send messages to each other. The last message had been from Chris saying he had the lighthouse key and they should meet on the viewing platform at two-thirty. He had asked her to wear the Horizon Ring.

It was case closed, but not as far as Kim was concerned.

'I don't care! Chris wouldn't do such a thing!' she said. 'He's not that kind of person.'

'Kim, you haven't seen him for years. You don't know what kind of person he's become.'

'Maybe I don't, but I know he's not like that! He used to

love Power Rangers!'

'I don't think a love of Power Rangers stops someone from being a killer.'

'Rosie,' Kim said, swallowing. 'Listen to me. Something is rotten here.'

'What makes you say that?'

Trixie whined and I stroked her head as Kim continued.

'Think of it this way,' she said. 'Chris supposedly murdered Katy Dark to steal the Horizon Ring, but somehow he's so inept that the best place he could hide it was under his pillow? And he lured Katy to that spot by sending a text message on a burner phone that *could be traced back to him*?'

I didn't reply. What Kim was saying was true. The dumbest criminal on Earth would hide the ring and dump both the phones. Was it possible he didn't have time? No. There were a thousand places at the inn where he could have hidden the ring, and he could have tossed both phones into the sea.

'That's true,' I said slowly. 'But he could have panicked.'

'Really? This isn't a crime of passion. The killer had a reason for taking a knife to the lighthouse. It wasn't to cut vegetables. Whoever killed Katy planned it. They didn't panic—and they certainly didn't hide the stolen ring under their pillow.'

'Okay. But I'm not sure what to do.'

'You've got to speak to Todd.'

'I'm not sure he'll listen to me.'

Todd had looked exceedingly pleased when Constable Turner had revealed the ring and told him about the phone. I doubted he'd want to hear that I thought they had the wrong man, especially as I had no evidence proving it.

Chris had been dragged away and tossed into the back of a police van as the media surrounded the vehicle, filming and snapping photos.

The expression on Chris's face had been—what? Surprise at being caught. Or something different? Confusion? Was Chris flat out dumbfounded by the discovery of the ring and the phone?

'We need to see him,' Kim said.

'I suppose so.' My best friend looked determined. I'd seen that look before as she'd run across the finishing line to win the Cape Carson marathon. It wasn't easy to dissuade Kim from something once her mind was made up. 'Although everything might not turn out as you want. Chris might confess. If he does, it's game over.'

Kim hesitated. 'If he confesses, then I'll live with that. But I bet he's innocent.'

We finished our coffees and headed to my car.

I felt exhausted. It seemed like a year had passed since the sun had risen. We drove across town and pulled up in front of the police station. After pushing through the media scrum, we made our way into the front office. A constable at the front desk glanced up.

'Media?' he said. 'You'll have to wait outside.'

'We're friends of Chris Dawson,' I said.

'I'm his girlfriend,' Kim added.

I gave her a sideways glance. That was a gross exaggeration, at the very least. Still, the desk constable didn't push it. He scribbled down our names and disappeared out the back, returning seconds later. 'Ten minutes,' he said. 'That's all.'

The constable made me leave Trixie in the waiting room before taking us to the cells. I'd been back here a few times over the years to speak to prisoners. The cells weren't like what you'd see in the movies: barred cages. They were rooms secured with metal doors. It still made no difference. Unless you had a stick of dynamite, once you were locked up, you weren't getting out.

A forlorn Chris sat on his bunk. His eyes turned to us. 'Thank goodness you're here.'

The constable reminded us again about the time limit and resecured the door. There weren't a whole lot of places to sit. Kim took the single chair opposite Chris while I sat beside him on the bunk.

'I'm innocent,' Chris continued. 'You have to believe that.'

'I believe you,' Kim said.

Oh dear, I thought.

There was no mistaking that lovelorn look on Kim's face.

You've got it bad, girl. If I hadn't been there, she probably would have thrown herself into his arms. We had no idea if Chris were guilty or innocent. We could be sitting opposite a callous murderer for all we knew.

'Chris,' I said. 'How did the ring get under your pillow? And the phone in your room?'

'Katy and I have had the phones for ages. We used them to keep our relationship secret from Cameron.'

'And the ring?'

Chris spread his hands. 'I don't know!' he said. 'It must have been planted!'

'We saw Katy and Chadek take the ring upstairs during dinner,' I said. 'They could have been lying, but why would Chadek and Katy do that?'

'They wouldn't,' Chris admitted. 'Katy was pedantic about keeping the ring secure. And Chadek's not dumb. He would have watched her put it into the safe with his own eyes.'

'Okay, but the text message told her to take the ring with her. Would you have ever asked her to do that?'

'Never. I'd seen the ring half a dozen times before. It was striking, but I would never ask her to bring it out with her, especially in the middle of the night.' He paused. 'Although, I suppose it was common knowledge that we met at odd hours.'

Kim cut in. 'The safe wasn't broken into,' she said. 'I heard one of the police talking about it. Katy took the ring with her.'

'The safe combination is set by the person renting the room,' I said. 'Do you know what Katy's combination would have been?'

'No,' Chris said. 'We never discussed that kind of thing.'

The other mystery was around the mobile phone. If Chris were telling the truth, someone who knew about the burner phone could have sent the message to Katy. It was possible. No one had worried too much about security. None of us had locked our rooms over the weekend. Someone could have put the phone back while everyone was searching. It would have only taken a minute.

My mind returned to the lighthouse.

Katy had been so happy the previous day. I remembered her expression. Something calm and carefree. How ironic it was that she would die in that same place only a few hours later. And her killer was probably someone who'd visited the lighthouse with her. We'd all stood on that same viewing gallery with her. Well, everyone except for Chris—

'Wait a minute,' I said, my mind returning to our group as we overlooked the ocean. 'Acrophobia.'

Chris stared at me. 'Pardon?'

'You were happy to switch rooms yesterday,' I said. 'It's quite a view from the room you'd been allocated. Yet you changed with Charlotte. The view from the other room is terrible; you can barely see anything. And you didn't go out onto the platform at the lighthouse. You didn't even leave the staircase.'

'I...well...'

'You have a fear of heights.'

Chris looked like a goldfish, his mouth silently opening and closing.

Kim was gazing at him too. 'You're right,' she said slowly. 'I remember that day on the beach years ago. A bunch of the guys dared each other to climb up the cliff. Chris, you only got halfway up before you stopped and turned back.'

'I...it's...it's true,' Chris said. 'I can't stand heights. It started when I was a kid. My dad was on the roof fixing loose tiles when he slipped and fell to the ground. He broke three ver-tebrae.' Chris swallowed. 'A therapist told me years later that I developed acrophobia because I saw the accident. I've always found heights so traumatising that I've never even been able to climb a ladder.'

The door to the cell opened, and the constable appeared.

'Time's up,' he said.

Kim and Chris exchanged a soulful glance. Before they could declare undying love for each other and arrange their wedding, I grabbed Kim by the arm and dragged her to the door.

'We'll be in touch,' I told Chris.

I didn't speak to Kim again until we'd retrieved Trixie and

reached the street.

'Chris wouldn't have gone out to meet Katy,' Kim said. 'It makes no sense.'

'Kim, he just admitted they used to meet at all times of the day and night.'

'True, but people having affairs usually met in hotels or in the back seats of cars. Not in local tourist attractions.'

Kim had a point. 'Although some people enjoy the risk of meeting up,' I pointed out. 'Anyway, I'll keep investigating. In the meantime, can you research Katy's career?'

'Sure,' Kim said. 'What am I looking for?'

'Was she really on an upward trajectory? Or was that just hype?'

'I'll do that.' She gave me a big hug. 'Thanks for everything.'

'Don't thank me yet.'

A feeling of apprehension crept over me as I watched Kim walk away. We still had plenty of unanswered questions.

If Chris didn't kill Katy Dark, then who did?

13

My phone rang.

'Rosie?' the voice came mellifluously over the line. 'Regina Lynch here.'

I rolled my eyes. Mayor Regina Lynch only ever rang me when she wanted something—and that was all too often.

Trixie looked up at me and whined.

I know how you feel, I thought.

'Regina?' I said.

'It's been so long!'

'It has,' I replied, unhappy that the interval had come to an end. 'What can I help you with?'

'It's all this business about death. It's so unpleasant, and at a time when we need to promote positive news stories.'

'Yes, but—'

'We need to talk.'

Isn't that what we're already doing?

'Okay,' I said.

'The Highgate hotel in an hour? Does that work for you?' Without waiting for an answer, Regina said she'd see me in the main bar by the window. 'They always save a table for me.'

'I suppose—'

The phone went dead. Groaning, I climbed into my jeep with Trixie at my side and turned to her.

'Looks like we're off to the pub,' I said.

Trixie barked.

'But first, I've got to go home,' I continued. 'I haven't even showered today, and I'm feeling like an old washcloth.'

We were soon back home, where I found Nan in the kitchen. The aroma of cakes cooking filled the whole house, and she was wearing her apron that read *I'm the Boss* on the front. She turned from the oven and put down a towel. 'Rosie!' she said. 'What's this I hear about Katy Dark getting murdered?'

I assured her it was true.

'My goodness.' Nan put on her oven mittens and removed a tray of cupcakes from the oven. 'And it was Kim's old boyfriend?'

'We're not so sure about that.' I quickly explained what we'd discovered about Chris and his fear of heights. 'Though it could still be him. Chris might have overcome his fear of heights, and he's just pretending it's still a problem.' Peering over her shoulder, I inhaled deeply. 'Hmm. They smell good.' Nan slapped my hand as I reached for one.

'Wait till they're iced,' she said. 'A cupcake without icing is like a day without sun.'

Laughing, I hurried to the bathroom, showered, and changed into a fresh pair of slacks and a new blouse. Despite the mayor not being one of my favourite people, I still needed to look professional. I gave Nan a quick *ta-ta* before racing to the car and driving across town to the Highgate.

It was late afternoon. Despite it being autumn, the day had turned unseasonably warm.

From years of living in Cape Carson, I knew rain often followed on the tail of a balmy autumn day. My thoughts turned to the lighthouse as I climbed from my jeep: the image of Katy's body, her outstretched hand, and the single letter written in her own blood.

C.

What does it mean?

Chris, Cameron, Colin, Charlotte, Cindy, or Chadek?

I left Trixie tied up on the footpath. Inside, I found Mayor Lynch—known to her detractors as Mayor Lunch because of her horrendously long lunches—sitting at a window overlooking the bay. She was an attractive woman in her fifties, slim with her hair in a blonde bob. Regina gave a girlish wave.

'Rosie Ryan!' she said. 'You look fabulous, darling. Just fabulous! And after such a trying day!'

'It has been a bit rough,' I admitted, sitting down. 'What are you drinking?'

'Lemon, lime and bitters. I've got to stay sober for the evening's festivities. Helping out at the high school. They're putting all the floats together for the parade.'

I'd seen Regina and her 'helping out' before. Charging in like a bull in a China shop, she usually told everyone what a great job they were doing and made an inordinate number of unhelpful suggestions before disappearing into the sunset.

I ordered a soft drink and listened while Regina detailed the town's events. 'Everything's running to schedule. The contest—well, you know all about that, you lucky girl! You're the judge! Then there's the parade. That'll be great fun. And the world record attempt with Spud Butler. It's inspiring!' She paused. 'Of course, we can't have everything getting derailed at the last moment. It would be like that shark movie.'

'Shark movie?'

'You know. The killer shark?'

'*Jaws*?'

'That's it. The town's looking forward to a big summer, and then a horrible big shark turns up and eats people. It's terrible timing.'

'Oh yes. If only they could have been eaten in the off-season.'

Oblivious to my sarcasm, Regina continued. 'That's why I'm so pleased that Katy's killer has been caught. Now we can get on with the Cupcake Festival and leave this unpleasantness behind.'

'Chris Dawson hasn't been found guilty yet,' I pointed out. 'There still has to be a trial and—'

'Trial!' Regina let out a peal of laughter. 'When has a trial ever brought more people to Cape Carson?'

'Everything isn't about bringing tourists.'

'Rosie,' Regina said, addressing me like a child. 'This town needs to grow. We need hotels. A marina. Did you know there are shops that sell only donuts? Can you believe it?'

'I can believe it,' I told her. 'You sound like Giuseppe Costa.'

The man owned properties all along the coast and was the most disliked person in town.

'Giuseppe has vision,' Regina said. 'A dream of what this town could be.'

More like a nightmare, I thought.

'Regina,' I said. 'Lots of people who live in Cape Carson don't want it to change. They want it to remain the same.'

'They're old sticks in the mud,' Regina said. 'Anyway, we need to focus on the here and the now: the Cupcake Festival. People come here from miles around to experience positivity and joy. Oh, and cupcakes.'

'Just because there's been a murder—'

'Dead people aren't fun, Rosie. Especially murdered ones.'

'They're not known for their humour.'

'All I'm saying is that I'd appreciate it if you could keep the story straight. Katie Dark's been murdered. It's bad luck, but at least her killer's been caught. We now have the Cupcake Festival to focus on.' She stood. 'I knew I could rely on you, Rosie. You're a true daughter of Cape Carson. And, never forget, we're building a legacy that will last a thousand years.'

'They said that about the Third Reich too.'

'Really?' She waved away my concern. 'I can never keep up with modern music. Give me The Carpenters any day.'

With a final *See you on the flipside,* Regina sailed out of the Highgate Hotel, leaving me to pay the bill. I gulped down the last of my soft drink.

'I hate that woman,' I muttered.

14

The scout hall was a frenzy of activity.

Women and men were everywhere. Some were laying out tablecloths on their designated tables. Others were setting up cupcake stands. A few were arranging lights and decorations around their tables to present their cupcakes when they finally went on display.

A woman arrowed towards me.

Oh no.

'Hello Ellen,' I said.

'Rosie Ryan!'

Ellen Whyte was a stout, older woman with a brisk manner. Her red hair was now greying, but age had not withered her. 'I must speak with you,' she said. 'It's about the judging.'

'Judging!'

The voice from the other side of the room belonged to Audrey Zouch, a thin sticklike woman who looked unerringly like the Wicked Witch from the Wizard of Oz. Audrey came scurrying over.

'Audrey,' I said. 'Is there a problem?'

'The only problem lies with those who wish to cheat,' Ellen snorted.

'Cheat?' Audrey snapped. 'Who are you calling a cheat?'

Ellen ignored her. 'It's about these tables—'

'Oh yes.' A man dashed over. Roger Ableman was the smallest of the three. Only five feet tall, he was rotund with thick curly black hair. 'Rosie! Thank heavens you've arrived. These women have been bullying me terribly.'

'Bullying!' Ellen snorted.

'Stay out of the kitchen if you can't take the heat!' Audrey added.

I held up my hands. 'Can someone tell me—*calmly*—what you're arguing about?'

Chaos reigned as they all spoke at once.

'Ellen,' I cut them off. 'You first.'

'It's the tables. They're completely unacceptable.'

I glanced at the tables. They'd been laid out in a herringbone pattern, as was agreed to with the Cupcake Committee. I tried, without success, to see something that would have aggravated the contestants.

'And the problem is...' I started.

Audrey spoke up. 'The selection process,' she said. 'It's in alphabetical order—by *surname*. All those with names that begin with earlier letters of the alphabet are at the front—'

'Which is no problem at all,' Roger interrupted.

I could understand why that suited Roger. The surname of Ableman put him in prime position. This wasn't the case for Ellen, whose last name of Whyte put her close to the back, and the situation was even worse for Audrey.

Her surname—Zouch—put her in the furthest corner from the front.

'Which *is* a problem,' Audrey retorted.

'Uh,' I said. 'That's not really a problem. The judging is based on the quality of the cupcake.'

'Phooey!' Ellen said. 'Did you just arrive in the last batch of dough, Rosie?'

'Er, no—'

'The judging is biased!'

'Everyone knows that!' Audrey added.

'Harry's been the contest judge for years,' I said. 'He would never show favouritism—'

'He picked one of his neighbours one year,' Roger said. 'The woman lived on his street—'

'And his technique was always sloppy,' Audrey cut in. 'He does the rounds of the tables, sampling one after another without pausing. By the time he reaches the last table, his taste buds are ruined. Deadened. *Decimated* by the taste of *inferior* cupcakes.'

'I'm sure that's not the case.' Harry had never mentioned decimated taste buds to me. 'Harry would do his best to be fair to everyone.'

'Absolutely,' Roger agreed.

Audrey turned to him. 'You would say that,' she said. 'Your table is first. Try changing your name to Zouch.'

'A tempting offer, but I think I'll stick to Ableman.'

'You would!'

'Listen,' I said, keen to nip this in the bud. 'Everyone, thank you for bringing this to my attention. I'm now aware that bias according to table position can occur, and I'll be on the lookout for it.'

'I doubt that will help,' Ellen said.

'Well,' I said, thinking. 'I suppose I could do the taste testing in reverse order. That way, the latter letters would be first.'

'Yes!' Audrey said.

'Yes!' Ellen agreed.

'No!' Roger said. 'That would be...I mean...it's never been done before. There are traditions...'

His voice trailed off, and I thought I may have won. But that was when another woman wandered over. 'What are you saying?' she asked.

The curious look on her face turned to hostility when I explained.

'What?' she said. 'You can't do that.'

'I'm just saying—'

I struggled to remember her name.

What is it? That's right. It's Natalie.

Oh, dear. Natalie *Borgen*.

Another woman appeared. 'What's happening?'

'They're talking about changing the order of the tables.'

'It means we'll be at the back,' Roger said, lowering his voice. 'The *fix* is in.'

'Fix?' I said blankly. 'I'm just trying to make it fairer.'

'For whom?' the newcomer asked. 'We all know the judges can't be trusted. Thank God they haven't got that Harry Bumshore—'

'Blackshore,' I corrected her firmly. 'And Harry's a very nice man.'

'—because I've never placed, and it's because I ran over his foot one day in my old Ford. I'm sure he stuck his foot out on purpose—'

I remembered the incident. Harry had worn a moon boot for a month after the accident. Who was this woman again? That's right—Angela *Douglas*.

Preparations were abandoned as the angrily crowd gathered, accompanied by cries of *she's changing the rules* and *Roger's a cheat,* and *she's already picked the winner.* Something flew through the air—a flying saucer—and not of the alien variety. It missed my head by an inch and smashed against the wall.

'Who threw that?' I demanded. 'That's not nice—'

The crowd grew louder. A trestle table was shoved. Some-one's hair was pulled. A cupcake stand was thrown.

Then things got *really* ugly.

15

'This will make you feel better,' Nan said. 'Tea always does.'

It had been a long day. The brawl at the scout hall had resulted in the breaking of two trestle tables, four black eyes, a sprained wrist, and the loss of Roger Ableman's toupee.

'I didn't even know he wore a hairpiece,' I told Nan.

'It must have been a very good one.'

'Constable Turner said he saw something floating in the gutter outside the hall after the fight. It may have been his toupee.'

Nan and I settled back with our cups of tea. I'd only taken a single, glorious sip when my phone rang. I sighed. 'Nan,' I said. 'Mobile phones are a blessing and a curse. They allow you to be contactable at all times.'

'Is that the blessing or the curse?'

'Both.' I glanced at the caller. *Oh, dear.* Wanda Gibson. This wasn't a conversation I was looking forward to.

'Hi Wanda,' I reluctantly answered.

'Greetings, Rosie. I understand there was an upset at the hall this afternoon.'

That was probably the understatement of the century.

Hesitantly, I told Wanda what had transpired, expecting her to admonish me for what had happened. Instead, she was surprisingly sympathetic.

'Being the Cupcake judge is a challenging role,' Wanda said. 'This is why people have always avoided doing it.'

'Thanks for being so understanding—'

'Which is why, Rosie, we *always* refer to the Cupcake Judging manual,' she said. 'Have you been reading it?'

I'd read the cover. I supposed that counted as reading it. 'Yes,' I said. 'Some of it.'

'Section Nine, Subsection Four, Paragraph two covers the allocation of tables to contestants. They are *always* allocated in alphabetical order.'

I reminded myself to give Ellen and Audrey black eyes to match the ones they already had. 'That simplifies things,' I admitted.

'Promise me you'll read the manual.'

'I promise.'

'Now, let me speak to Nan. She has a recipe for lemon meringue pie that I simply must have.'

After wishing her goodnight, I passed my phone to Nan, and the women chatted for a while before hanging up. I gave an enormous yawn.

'You need to sleep,' Nan said.

'Is that an order?'

'Absolutely.'

Grumbling that I was a grown woman and could make my own decisions, I headed to the bedroom, stripped off, and climbed into bed. I was aware of Trixie taking up her spot on the floor beside me. Then sleep came, and I knew nothing more until I awoke to sunlight streaming through my window.

I glanced at the time.

8.05 am.

'Good grief,' I muttered. 'I really must have needed a rest.'

Checking my phone, I found I already had several messages, including one from Harry.

Heard you created a sensation at the scout hall. Stay with the Katy Dark story and see where it takes you.

I nodded thoughtfully. I'd discovered a lot the previous day. Working out what to do next wasn't easy. Not only had no one broken down and confessed to the killing, everyone's story had been plausible.

The other message was from Colin.

Feel like a coffee this morning? I've had thoughts about Katy's death.

I wasn't sure how to react. He'd seemed a little *too* friendly the previous day.

And short men were not my thing. I always felt like Gulliver wandering about in the land of the Lilliputians.

Deciding that not replying was the best course of action for the moment, I headed to the kitchen. Nan had been up for hours. She'd already done her yoga for the day. Despite being eighty-three years old, she was one of the most flexible people I knew.

'Just in time for breakfast!' she said, waving a bowl of cereal at me.

'Gosh,' I said, peering into her bowl. 'What's in there? You've got everything except the nuts and bolts.'

'You get your iron through other sources,' Nan quipped. 'I've got oats. Raisins. Nuts. Blueberries. Banana. Chia seeds. Apple—'

'I get the idea.'

She quickly threw together a similar bowl for me. We grabbed cups of tea and headed to the backyard. Settling onto a garden seat, I took a deep breath. *This is so beautiful.* The morning sun cast great shards of bright, early light across the huge eucalypts that overlooked our place. Birds flitted and soared from branch to branch as we silently ate.

My mind went back to the events of the previous day. I thought back to the dinner. Katy laughing so gaily. Everyone heading off to bed. Waking during the night. Seeing Katy leave the building. Finding her body at the top of the lighthouse.

Her outstretched hand with the letter *C* scrawled onto the metal deck.

I'm missing something.

I knew it in my gut. In the events of the last two days, something didn't quite make sense, and I had no idea what. After finishing my breakfast, I picked up my phone and sent a text.

That would be great, Colin. Nine-thirty at Sandy's Diner okay?

His answer came back almost immediately.

Great. See you there.

Thanking Nan for breakfast, I grabbed our crockery and took it inside. Then, after showering, I decided to take Trixie for a quick walk. By then, Nan was back at the jigsaw puzzle, putting in some pieces that looked like they were part of the Coliseum.

'How's it going?' I asked.

'You know what they say.'

'Not *again*.'

'Rome wasn't built in a day!'

'Really? I hadn't heard that before.'

Heading out the door with Trixie, we headed down our street and onto the forest trail that led to Cut Rock Lookout. Being surrounded by nature was a welcome break after the previous day's events.

There's something about nature that really does soothe the soul. The weather was warm, and the bush was still. A superb fairywren flitted between some bottlebrush and came to rest on a low-lying branch.

'Hey you,' I said softly.

Trixie barked, and the bird disappeared into the undergrowth. Laughing, I continued on to the headland. A few people were already there, looking out at the sea.

Surfers were taking advantage of the waves around at Shelly Beach. A jogger raced past me. Seagulls wheeled on the breeze. The ocean rushed into the giant split in the rock, sending a cascade of spray into the air.

I gazed out at the ocean. The water was calm, and the sun sparkled on it like diamonds. A mass of birds trailed a fishing boat about a kilometre off the coast. Sucking in another breath of fresh air, I cast my gaze towards the town. People were already up and about. The streets were busy. For all the conflict it caused, the Cupcake Festival brought people to town. Lots of them. My gaze settled on its famous lighthouse.

Or infamous, maybe. But I hoped not. I didn't want it only remembered as the place where Katy Dark died.

'Hey!' a voice called.

My daughter and her husband Tom were out for a jog. They angled towards me. They were sporty people, usually dividing their attention between swimming and rock climbing. At first, their interest in scaling great heights had scared me silly, but I felt better after they'd explained all the safety procedures.

This jogging business was a new hobby.

'So the rumours are true,' I said. 'You've become hot, sweaty people who are in a terrible hurry to get nowhere.'

'Mum. That's the most terrible description of jogging that I've ever heard.'

'But true,' Tom added.

Amanda seemed to be coping better than her husband. She was red-faced, but Tom had turned beetroot. 'He's an old bloke,' she said, smiling. 'That's why he can't keep up.'

Tom was twenty-five, only two years old than her. 'I know,' he said. 'My weary, aching bones. Time to put me out to pasture.'

I grinned. 'Tom might still have a couple of good years left.'

'Fair enough.' Amanda wrapped an arm around his sweaty waist. 'I might keep him.'

'Good of you,' Tom said. 'Give me a rock face to climb any day.'

'I can still scale a cliff faster than you with one hand tied behind my back.'

'Liar!'

Laughing, they said goodbye and ran off down the hill towards town. Watching them go, I felt inordinately pleased that Amanda was so happy. They worked as real estate agents in town and were good at it. No grandkids had appeared yet, and it hadn't come up in conversation.

Oh well, I thought. *Everything in its time.*

I glanced at my watch.

Talking about time...

'Come on,' I said to Trixie. 'Let's go.'

Back at home, I grabbed my bag and changed my shoes before heading out again in my jeep. I pulled up in front of Sandy's Diner a few minutes later, where I found Colin waiting. He was already seated at a table facing the beach, nursing a glass of water. He jumped up and kissed my cheek as I sat down.

'Rosie!' he said. 'Nice to see you survived yesterday's ordeal.'

'It was quite a day.'

A girl who worked at the diner came out to take our order. Colin ordered a cappuccino while I asked for my usual coffee.

'A jumbo double-shot caramel latte?' Colin said, raising an eyebrow. 'That must pack quite a wallop!'

'I'm like the walking dead until I've had one.'

Our drinks arrived, and I greedily took a sip of my coffee.

Heaven!

'This is a lovely town you've got here,' Colin said. 'It seems quite busy.'

'It's because of the festival.'

'Oh, yes: the Cupcake Festival. Quite a clever idea, really.

Must bring lots of tourists.'

'It does.' I wasn't here to talk about the festival; I wanted to discover what Colin knew. 'So you mentioned that you'd had some thoughts about Katy's murder.'

'It's just something I remembered about that girl at the hotel. The one in the bar.'

'Dorothy?'

'That's right. I glanced out my window just before I got into bed. Dorothy was walking to that outbuilding she lives in.'

'The bungalow?'

'She seemed upset. I thought nothing of it at the time.'

I remembered spotting Dorothy with Cameron in the hall. What were they talking about?

'—*can't do anything for you,*'

'*But I came all this way to see you.*'

'*Then you've wasted your time!*'

Cameron had called her an autograph hunter. He could have been tired and irritable and refused an autograph. But that wouldn't explain her saying *I came all this way to see you*. She was already working at the inn. And would a simple refusal cause her to be that upset?

Now that I thought about it, Chris was arrested before we finished interviewing everyone. There were two people we hadn't spoken to. One was Jason Rodd. Sheila said he lived in Barkly. The other was Dorothy.

'Thanks,' I said to Colin. 'That's helpful. I'll follow up on it.'

'Do you mind if I ask a favour?'

'Sure. What?'

'Can I take a look at your bag? I've never seen one like it.'

Laughing, I handed it over. 'This is *incredible*,' he said. 'They should make these for men.'

'You must really love bags!'

'It's the pockets! I've always loved bags with lots of pockets!'

That was a fetish I could understand. Laughing, I playfully dragged the bag away from him. 'Get your own!' I said.

He grinned. 'Rosie,' he said. 'I'm going to be staying here for a few more days. Can I ask another favour?'

'What is it?'

'It would be helpful to have a guide. Someone to show me around.'

I wasn't sure if he wanted a guide or a girlfriend. Either way, I didn't want to offend him. He seemed like a pleasant man. Short, and not my type, but pleasant.

'I'm pretty busy,' I said.

'Is it the Cupcake Festival?'

'I'm afraid so.'

'You're choosing cupcakes over me?'

'They *are* iced,' I pointed out.

We laughed again as I finished my coffee and glanced at my

watch. 'Better get moving,' I said. 'I've got a million things to do.'

'The coffee's my shout,' Colin said.

'Fine. It's my shout next time.'

16

I walked in the door of the Gazette just in time to see Doris putting the phone down.

'Hello stranger,' she said. 'Heard you had some excitement.'

'Depends on what you mean by excitement. I almost get beaten up at the local scout hall and a famous actress gets mysteriously murdered. Those kinds of excitement I can do without.' I glanced towards Harry's office. 'Is he in?'

'No, he had an appointment with the bank.'

One of Harry's roles as editor-in-chief was handling the budget and ensuring the Gazette stayed in the black. The newspaper always walked a fine line between solvency and liquidation. Heading out to my office, I found Ellie helping Jay with something on his computer. Considering Jay spent all his spare time playing video games, it always surprised me how illiterate he was with computers. I sat at my desk and opened a new document.

'Has Jay broken his computer again?' I asked.

Trixie gave an accompanying groan.

'I'm afraid so,' Ellie said. 'Jay thought there were eligible singles in his area wanting to date him, he clicked on the ad, and he now has a nasty little virus installed.'

'Jay,' I said. 'Can't you use a dating app like everyone else?'

'That doesn't sound very romantic.'

'You old softie. There are a thousand women in this town, Jay.'

'Really?'

'Yes. Stop playing computer games and go out and meet some.'

Ellie finally purged the virus from Jay's computer, and I settled down to make notes about what had happened at the Lighthouse Inn.

I transcribed everything people had said during the interviews, creating a timeline of events to keep everything clear in my head. Peering at it, I realised there was a fairly obvious gap.

I rang Todd Parker.

'Rosie,' he said, answering. 'You haven't started another brawl, have you?'

'No. I'm working up to it. Anyway, I have a question about the text message sent to Katy's phone.'

'Really? I have questions too. Like where do all those missing socks go? And how do you get the last of the toothpaste out of the tube?'

'Todd, you're hilarious—not. I could ask Chris, but you've inconveniently stuck him in a jail cell.'

Todd sighed. 'Probably because he murdered someone,' he said. 'We tend to do that with killers.'

'I'd like to know what time the text message was sent to Katy.'

'That information's part of an ongoing police investigation.'

'Didn't you just say it had been solved?'

Todd groaned. 'All right,' he said. 'I'll do you a favour. It was sent after midnight.'

'When—exactly?'

'Twelve twenty-five, to be exact. Why do you want to know?'

I explained about Chris having a fear of heights. It seemed likely that someone else had committed the murder and pinned it on him.

'Really?' Todd said. 'You think Chris is innocent?'

'Kim thinks he is.'

Todd laughed. 'So you think we should release him?' He paused. 'Rosie, someone with a fear of heights can still commit murder. And the evidence is compelling. Chris's burner phone was found with the message arranging the meeting with Katy. He also had the stolen diamond ring in his room.'

'Keeping the ring under his pillow was a pretty lame place to hide it.'

'True. But criminals aren't known for their smarts, and

Chris wasn't expecting us to search the rooms.'

'What about the threatening letter found on Katy's pillow?'

'Probably just a ruse on Chris's part to divert attention from himself.'

'Hmm.'

'Now,' Todd said. 'While I've got your attention, are you doing anything Sunday night?'

'I might be available.' Todd and I had gone out on a few dates, and our relationship could best be described as friendly. 'What did you have in mind?'

'Dinner. And maybe a walk along the shore.'

Hmm. An evening stroll along the beach with a big handsome hunky guy. What wasn't there to like about that? I said yes and told Todd we could make a time later. Putting my phone down, I saw Jay staring at me.

'What?' I said.

'You make it look so easy.'

'It is easy. Just relax. And keep an open mind about those dating apps.'

'What's the one you used?'

'*Ideally Yours*? They closed. One of the partners stole all the money and ran off to South America.'

I glanced at my watch. It was almost lunchtime.

After updating my notes, I headed down to Percy Street with Trixie to grab some food. I'd almost reached the diner when I glanced across the road and spotted a familiar figure.

Chadek.

I frowned. The Russian wore a pair of sunglasses and a cap. He looked like a bad actor in a spy film. I was caught between my curiosity and my growling stomach. After a brief battle between brain and body, my brain won. Chadek strode east, obviously in a hurry.

It only took me a moment to realise he was heading for one of the beachside car parks. If he jumped into a vehicle and drove off, I'd lose him and never discover why he was looking so suspicious. I broke into a run, headed back up Kerr Street where my jeep was parked and jumped in.

Trixie gave an excited bark as I did a U-turn, scraping my hubcaps on the gutter, and drove back down to Percy Street.

Where is he?

My eyes scanned the car park. Was I wrong about where he'd been heading? No. *There he is.* The black SUV was driving west down Percy street. I followed a discreet distance behind. The road passed the lighthouse where it turned onto Millicent Drive. This was one long undulating stretch of tar with the sand dunes of West Beach on one side and thick bush on the other. Knowing I stood out like a sore thumb, I allowed another car to overtake me.

'I wonder where he's going,' I said to Trixie. 'The only thing along here is sand.'

This road went to Port Logan, a tiny spot even quieter than Cape Carson. After that, it angled inland, where it eventually met the highway. From there, you could head west to South Australia or back to Melbourne.

'If he's doing a runner,' I muttered, 'he's going about it in a very roundabout way.'

The SUV indicated and turned left down a side road for the beach. I slowed and pulled to a stop at the turnoff. There were dozens of these places along this section of the coast: tiny car parks where you could park and walk the beach. They were also remote spots where anything could happen.

Was this a trap? Had Chadek spotted me in his rear-view mirror and was drawing me in like a fly into a web? Was he in the car park, waiting to kill me?

That seemed farfetched. Chadek had no reason to kill me. Still, there was a better way to see what was going on. Moving the jeep to a spot under an overhanging tea tree, I took to the road on foot with Trixie by my side. It was only a few hundred feet down to the beach. The road was winding, and I could dive into the bushes if I heard an approaching car.

Coming around a final bend, I saw Chadek and the black SUV. A dark-grey Audi with tinted windows was parked nearby. An onshore breeze wafted in from the shimmering ocean beyond.

Chadek was next to the Audi, leaning near the window to

converse with someone behind the wheel. A few of his words were being carried by the breeze, but they were spoken in Russian.

Then the man in the car said something forcefully, a word that sounded like *vorovat*. Chadek said something in reply, his arms spread in protest.

A shot rang out.

17

'Trouble seems to follow you everywhere,' Todd Parker said.

'It's one of my most endearing qualities,' I replied.

'If you say so.'

We were in the car park where Chadek had been shot. A quick call to 000 had brought both an ambulance and the police. After the shooting, I'd leapt into the bushes with Trixie as the grey vehicle took off at high speed. Then I'd raced over to Chadek to find the bodyguard lying in a pool of his own blood.

One paramedic had described Chadek's condition as serious before he was taken away in the ambulance. The next few hours had passed slowly, with Todd taking a statement from me while the other officers combed the scene for evidence.

'So you're sure you don't know what the conversation was about?' Todd asked.

'They were too far away from me,' I said. 'I couldn't really hear anything—plus Chadek was speaking in Russian.'

'And your Russian's not great?'

'The only Russian word I know is Vodka.' I thought for a moment. 'There was one word I did catch, Todd, though I can't remember what it was.' I searched my brain. 'Hang on a minute. The word was *vorovat*.'

'And that means?'

I checked my phone. 'To steal or pilfer.'

Todd frowned. 'I wonder how that fits with Katy Dark's death.'

'No idea.' I dived in. 'Although the smart thing would be for you to release Chris and work with me to solve Katy's murder.'

'Nice try, although I think I'll keep Chris Dawson locked up because all the evidence points to him.'

'If you say so.'

I drove back to town. By now, my head was aching, and it wasn't just because of stress. I'd had only one coffee, and my caffeine level had dropped to a dangerously low level. It was amazing that I was still functional.

After parking the car, I slumped into one of the front tables at Sandy's, where she came out to serve me. 'Coffee,' I grunted.

'Sounds like you're in a bad way.'

'The worst. If I die from caffeine deprivation, tell my family I love them, and tell Kim she can keep my DVD copy of *Gone With The Wind*.'

Trixie nuzzled my hand while I waited. 'Yes, I know I'm

addicted,' I said, slipping her one of my homemade doggy snacks. 'Don't hassle me.'

Coffee soon magically appeared, and I settled back to drink it. In the space of a few days, I'd seen the dead body of Katy Dark and watched a man get shot. It was a lot to take in. I closed my eyes. The day was almost done, and I felt like going to sleep. Fortunately, the only thing I had to do tonight was familiarise myself with the cupcake judging manual.

There was movement at my side: Sandy. 'Hey Rosie,' she said. 'I just remembered. This was left for you earlier.'

She handed me an envelope with my name on it.

'Do you know who left it?' I asked.

'No idea. I went out the back for a moment and found it on the counter.'

Sandy returned to the kitchen. Frowning, I tore open the envelope to find it contained a single sheet of paper. I read:

I have important information about a serious crime.

Meet me in the RSL Club's underground car park at six o'clock.

Come alone.

Open-mouthed, I put down the letter.

There was no signature or indication of who had sent it. It wasn't often that I got anonymous tips, but it did happen. Someone either had information about Katy Dark's murder or Chadek's shooting.

I glanced at my watch.

Sheesh! No wonder I felt like a wreck. It was almost six o'clock; I'd had a stressful day and barely eaten anything. After gulping down the last of my coffee, I paid up and was soon driving to the Cape Carson Returned & Services League Club.

It would be great to say that all RSL clubs were outstanding, architecturally-designed buildings that truly paid homage to our returned soldiers. In reality, most were great, a lot were fine, but a few were downright ugly. Unfortunately, the Cape Carson branch fell into the latter category. The place was a two-storey brick joint on Donovan Street. It had been built back in the sixties when big square buildings with aluminium windows were all the rage, although how that had ever been popular always baffled me.

I'd been there a few times over the years, and it was as worn out as some of the people who frequented it. The carpet was old, the place reeked of stale alcohol, and the lighting was subdued, probably to hide the stained wallpaper on the walls. One-armed bandits, cheap booze, meat raffles, and specialty dance nights were the only things that kept it going.

In front was a small memorial to our soldiers. The entrance to the underground car park was down the side of the building at the end of a narrow graffiti-strewn alley. Creeping down in my jeep, I followed the ramp under the building and slotted into a tight spot in the underground basement.

Trixie gave a whine as I turned off the engine. Down here was quiet, but a faint thrum came from above. Music. Feet on floors. The restaurant. Maybe it was relatively cheerful up there, but down here, the atmosphere could best be described as post-apocalyptic. Half the fluorescents were out with one corner in absolute darkness. The place stunk of garbage and cigarettes.

What a great place for a murder.

A vehicle's engine roared to life. Headlights flared, and it took off, an old pensioner behind the wheel. He weaved unsteadily up the ramp and disappeared from view. I swallowed. Checked my watch. Six o'clock. Where was the person who'd sent the letter? Was this a trap? Maybe this whole thing was a ruse to kill me.

Trixie barked.

'What is it, girl?' I asked.

Then a section of darkness in the corner broke away, and a silhouette appeared. The figure took refuge behind a column. Leaving Trixie in the car, I got out and cautiously manoeuvred between the vehicles.

'Don't come any closer,' the person ordered.

The voice was so raspy that I couldn't tell if it was male or female.

'Who are you?' I asked.

'That's not important, but you can call me...Voicebox.'

Voicebox? What kind of name is that?

'Okay,' I said uncertainly. Before I could say anything more, another vehicle came down the ramp, its headlights flared, and Voicebox shrank into the shadows. A woman got out of her car and took the elevator upstairs.

My eyes searched the darkness. 'Why did you send me that message?'

The dark figure peered around the corner. 'I've seen things,' Voicebox rasped. 'Illegal things.'

'What do you mean?'

'There are crimes that must be punished.'

'Crimes?' Were they referring to Katy Dark's murder and the attempt on Chadek's life? 'What do you mean?'

'Poison.'

Poison?

'You're saying someone is going to be killed with poison?'

Voicebox growled. 'Yes.'

'Who?' I demanded. 'How? When?'

'The cupcakes are poisonous.'

'What?'

'Far too much sugar,' Voicebox continued. 'And vanilla essence instead of *real* vanilla. Ellen Whyte and Audrey Zouch never use the best ingredients—'

I darted forward, grabbed Voicebox's arm, and dragged him into the light.

'Roger?' I yelled.

'Oh dear,' the little man muttered, red-faced. 'I wish you hadn't done that.'

I released him. 'What on earth are you doing?' I demanded. 'I thought you had something serious to tell me!'

'I do! Poorly made cupcakes give this town a bad name. And both Ellen and Audrey's are the worst. They never use the best ingredients. It's always cheap sugar and margarine instead of butter—'

'But...but...I thought someone...I mean...poison...' I looked harder at Roger Ableman. He had a black eye and was sans toupee. 'You can't make allegations like this.'

'But I want to win the contest!'

'That's no excuse!'

'I've been entering for twenty years—and never even placed!'

'Then you need to try harder.' I felt sorry for the man. He looked so unhappy, especially without his hairpiece. 'Do you have a good recipe?'

'I always use my mother's recipes.'

'Really?' I remembered something Nan had mentioned about Roger. A tax accountant, he had lived with his mother, Lorraine, his whole life until her death a few years before. Nan had said that Lorraine was about as good as a cook as Nan was a sharpshooter—and Nan had never fired a gun in her life.

'Maybe it's time to change.'

'But my mum's recipes—'

'We've all got to change with the times,' I said firmly. 'You're a member of the library?'

'Well, yes...'

'They've got a huge selection of cookbooks, including ones dedicated to specialty cupcakes. If what you've been doing hasn't worked, then it's time for something new.'

Roger slowly nodded. 'I suppose it's worth a try.'

'Good. Now let's get out of here. It sounds like it's Polka night upstairs—and I don't like Polkas!'

18

The next day took me back to the Lighthouse Inn.

Another clear day had dawned, and the early morning sun was so bright that it hurt to look at it. I shielded my eyes as I climbed from my trusty jeep with Trixie at my side, and headed for the inn. The visiting media pack had left. Their attention had shifted to the jail now that Katy's killer had been found. I found Sheila going through some paperwork at the front desk.

'Rosie,' she said. 'I heard about Chadek. Is he going to be all right?'

I told her the last I'd heard was that he would survive. 'He's a lucky man,' I said. 'Well, apart from getting shot.'

'Why was he shot?'

'No idea,' I said. 'I'm just heading up to my room.'

'Then I should mention that we weren't able to do a clean of the rooms yesterday. The police wouldn't allow it.'

I nodded. Heading upstairs, the grandfather clock gonged mournfully at me as I let myself into my room. Despite never having had an opinion about grandfather clocks, I was feeling less enthusiastic about them by the day.

Something's wrong.

I'd left my belongings here knowing that I'd return to the hotel. Now my decision to do that felt like a bad idea. My eyes took in my overnight bag, the bed, dressing table, and chest of drawers. It all had a slightly *disturbed* feel to it. I knew how I usually kept my living space, and there was something slightly *off* about this. I got Todd on the phone.

He answered almost immediately. 'Hey, Rosie.'

'Did you or your guys do a search of my room?'

'No. Should we? Are you confessing to something?'

'If I commit any crimes,' I said, 'you'll be the first to know.'

Thanking him, I hung up and went through my things one at a time. Everything was there though my suspicions were correct. I was in the habit of not zipping up my bag completely and not closing my drawers all the way. Some would call that sloppy; I think of it as endearing. Anyway, all my drawers were firmly shut, as was the zipper on my bag. I'd left my toiletries bag in the bathroom, and even this was secured.

Who would have come in here? I cast my mind back to the previous day. In the craziness of everything, I'd left my room unlocked. It hadn't worried me at the time. There were police everywhere. Someone, however, had searched my room.

But—for what?

All my money was in my handbag. Although I'd left some jewellery lying about, none of it was missing.

So who could have done it? There were the members of *The Six Cees*: Cameron, Cindy, Colin, Chris, Charlotte, and Chadek. Then there were the police officers who'd searched the hotel. One of them could have come into my room inadvertently. That left the inn's staff: Sheila Birdwhistle, Dorothy Stuart and Jason Rodd.

There was little I could do about solving this particular conundrum. However, it did remind me that I hadn't spoken to Jason yet. Or Dorothy. Heading downstairs, I found the assistant manager cleaning benchtops in the kitchen. She was strangely silent when I asked her about the conversation with Cameron.

'It was nothing,' she said, averting her eyes. 'I asked for an autograph.'

'And he said no?'

She nodded.

'You didn't see anything else that night?' I asked.

Dorothy sighed. 'There was something,' she said. 'I didn't mention this to the police. Sometimes, I don't sleep well. I heard a sound come from the inn. I got up and saw someone leaving.'

'About what time?'

'Sometime after two-thirty. Maybe a quarter to three. The

person was heading for Mermaid Point.'

'You couldn't see who it was?'

'No.'

'Male or female?'

'I really don't know.' She thought for a moment. 'Although the person had a larger build. It might have been a man. Anyway, he was carrying a bag.'

'Did you see him return?'

'Yes, about twenty minutes later. There was no bag when he came back.'

I quizzed her further, but there was nothing more she could add. After thanking her, I decided to take a walk to Mermaid Point. It was a lovely spot only a few hundred metres past the lighthouse toward West Beach. It overlooked a circular break in the rock platform known as the Cauldron. It was a constant, churning mass of water sloshing about in all directions. In the middle was a tiny rocky island upon which sat our local mermaid.

Well, that's how we thought of her. Nicknamed Ariel, the mermaid was actually a lump of rock that resembled a reclining woman, a rocky hand raised to shield her eyes as she peered out to sea.

A guard rail ran all the way along the cliff face, although it was presently in a state of disrepair. A section was missing, and hazard tape and warning signs had been put up to keep people back. I seemed to recall hearing that a woman had died after falling from here many years ago.

Although it seemed insane that anyone would willingly jump in here, there was no shortage of crazy people. Several people had been injured over the years. Scuba diving was also a bad idea.

I peered gloomily into the swirling water. A guest from the inn had disposed of something during the night. They could have thrown it in anywhere along the coast, but—if they were trying to hide something—this spot was the most likely. It was only a few minutes from the inn, and the chances of anyone ever recovering it were virtually zero.

As to what they'd disposed of, I had no idea. It wasn't the murder weapon. The knife had remained in the middle of Katy Dark's chest.

So what was it?

My phone rang. *Kim.* I told her briefly what I'd discovered, and her opinion was the same as mine when it came to retrieving the item.

'You'd have to be mad,' she said. 'At least three people have drowned there over the years.'

Kim's specialty as a librarian was in local history.

'Three?' I said. 'I only knew about one.'

'The other two were decades ago. The last one was a few years back. Even on a calm day, the currents beneath the surface can be ferocious.'

I thought again about what had been tossed in there. Whatever it was could hold the key to everything.

'Have you had any luck with the research?' I asked.

'Some,' Kim said. 'You know that new movie that Katy was working on?'

'*The President's Robot*?'

'Apparently, it was going to be big. Really big. Some major stars would be involved with it. Katy's paycheck was to be twenty million plus a percentage of the profits.'

'Wow.' I thought about this. 'So Katy was about to come into a fortune. That would seem to rule out Cameron as her killer.'

'And Cindy. It would be like killing the goose that laid the golden egg.' She continued. 'By the way, I heard some good news about Chadek. Apparently, he's conscious.'

'How'd you find that out?'

'I passed one of the women from the Storytime group when I was on my morning run.' During Storytime, books were read aloud to young children at the library. 'She works as a nurse at the hospital.'

'Really?' Finding out what Chadek knew would help a lot. 'Thanks for that. Chat later!'

Hanging up, I hurried back to my jeep with Trixie in tow and headed across town.

Cape Carson's public hospital is a small hospital by big-city standards.

Nestled in the shallow hills to the southwest of the town centre, the hospital can service up to fifty-five people. The single, two-storey building has various departments, including a prenatal unit, physio services, and a respite care section.

I pulled into the car park, leaving Trixie in my jeep before heading to reception. It wasn't until I had reached the front desk when I noticed the police officer. He was standing in one of the doorways. It didn't take a genius to work out he was there to protect Chadek. Someone had already tried to kill the Russian; they might try again. I recognised the girl at the front desk as Belinda. I'd interviewed her once for a story about hospital funding. After some pleasantries, I spied a bunch of files on the counter's edge. I glanced about. 'I'm supposed to be meeting someone here,' I said. 'Although it doesn't look like they've turned up—' Swinging my arm about, I knocked the stack of files onto the floor. 'Oh my goodness! I'm so sorry!'

Still apologising profusely, I stepped back as the policeman and Belinda stooped to gather all the paperwork. I scooted up the main corridor.

Where is he?

Two nurses wheeling a hospital gurney came around the corner. 'Coming through,' one of them said.

The gurney's occupant was a very pregnant woman who I

recognised immediately. 'Hi, Joy!' I said. 'It's time?'

'Past time,' she moaned, red-faced. 'I want this kid out—now!'

Joy worked part-time at Hogan's Sweets on Percy Street. She was the size of a house. No wonder she wanted it all over and done with. I scurried down the hall, trying to work out where Chadek would be recuperating.

Probably one of the private rooms. After checking half a dozen of these, I was beginning to lose hope when I stuck my head in through one door and saw him propped up in bed.

'Chadek!' I said. 'How are you going?'

He rolled his eyes. 'Oh,' he said in his guttural Russian accent. 'It's you.'

I could see this would require a more nuanced approach. 'Is there anything you need?' I asked. 'Magazines? Chocolates? Books?'

'I need to be left alone.'

Ignoring that, I settled onto the chair beside him. 'Chadek, you owe me something.'

'How do you work that out?'

'I saved your life. You were bleeding badly after you were shot. You would have died if I hadn't been there.'

He hesitated. 'I thank you for your help, but I cannot speak to you.'

'Why not?'

'If I told you, I would certainly be dead.'

'In that case, you need all the help you can get.'

Chadek looked away from me and peered out the window. A bird was dancing about on the tree outside. It gave a final cry before taking flight and disappearing from view.

'All I can say is that I had nothing to do with Katy's death,' he said.

'So why were you shot?'

He shrugged. 'I owed money to some people,' he said. 'Some *bad* people. They wanted it paid back, and I couldn't do it.'

This sounded like typical small-time gangster stuff. 'Do you know who killed Katy?'

'No.' Chadek hesitated. 'But my father was a jeweller, and I saw the ring after the police found it under Chris's pillow.'

'And...'

'You should have it checked out.'

'The ring? What do you mean?'

But he would say no more.

19

'It's fake,' Carlos Windermere said, removing the monocular from his eye. 'It's a very good fake, but it's still a fake.'

Todd's mouth dropped. It was fun to watch, especially seeing as how he'd resisted me every step of the way when I asked to have the Horizon Ring examined. First, he'd threatened to have me arrested for circumventing security at the hospital and speaking to Chadek. Then he'd flat out refused to have the ring checked. It was only when I dragged Carlos away from his jewellery shop in Donovan street and into the police station that Todd relented.

'Are you sure?' Todd finally asked.

Carlos smiled. He was sixty years old with short grey hair and a silvery Dali moustache. Despite his Spanish-sounding name, Carlos was as Australian as a meat pie. 'I've been doing this for forty years,' he said. 'It's cubic zirconia. I could run a multitude of tests, but I can already see several issues. The nearer facets are sharp. The ones at the back of the gem are blurred. That's because of high birefringence in the zircon.' He blew hot air on the ring's surface. 'Also, the stone remains fogged after I've breathed on it. That doesn't happen with diamonds.'

'But the ring looks like gold.'

'That's because it *is* gold,' Carlos said. 'That's what makes it all the more convincing, Rosie. Someone's gone to enormous trouble. The shank—the actual ring section—is extremely good quality gold. They've probably spent about a thousand dollars to create the shank and then spent a lot more on recreating the gemstone.'

I decided it was time to chime in. 'Can you tell how long ago it was made?'

He peered at the ring again. 'I can't say for sure,' he said. 'But the stone is unblemished. I'd say it was cut in the last year. The shank has been purposely burnished to make it look older.' He shook his head. 'It's an impressive forgery. The best I've ever seen.'

We thanked Carlos for his time, and he left.

'Wow,' I said. 'A fake ring. So when was the real ring stolen?'

Todd frowned. 'Katy and Cameron had the ring revalued the day before they left for Cape Carson,' he said.

'Could it have been swapped over at the jeweller's shop?'

'Unlikely. The place has been in business for a hundred and twenty years. And it was in Katy's possession from that time to when she arrived in Cape Carson.'

'You know that Katy's will leaves the ring to a cousin?'

'I know. What I'm wondering is how Chadek knew the ring was fake. Did Katy say something? Or was he involved in the swap?' He rubbed his chin. 'Chris mustn't have known he was stealing a fake ring when he killed Katy.'

I groaned. 'Let me get this straight,' I said. 'Chris, who has a fear of heights, arranges to meet Katy at the top of a lighthouse. He kills her, steals the ring—real or otherwise—and hides it in the most obvious place of all.'

'Stranger things have happened.'

'I give up,' I said, frustrated. 'I'll see you later.'

'Don't be like that.'

'Sorry. I've got to get my nails done.'

Todd tried to speak, but I stormed out of his office. The sky had turned cobalt blue, and a gusty breeze was blowing from the sea. The tempestuous weather matched my mood. I was angry with Todd. Despite handing him a major break, he was still clinging to this silly notion that Chris was responsible.

With Trixie at my side, I made my way down to the corner and took a deep breath. I needed to think clearly. This whole case was very confusing—or it wasn't. Not if Todd was right, and Chris killed Katy before stealing the Horizon Ring. Maybe I was reading too much into this. Kim could be wrong. The funny young teenage guy she'd enjoyed that romantic summer with all those years ago might have grown into a callous killer.

'What do you think?' I asked Trixie. 'Do people really change that much?'

She whined and rubbed her head against my leg. Trixie could always tell when I was unsettled. I dropped to one knee and rubbed her head. 'I love you, girl,' I said. 'Sometimes, I think you're the only one who understands me.'

Trixie barked.

We went back to my car. I had just climbed behind the wheel when my phone beeped. It was a message from Wanda.

Are you running late?

I stared at it. 'Oh no,' I said. 'It can't be tonight.'

Panicked, I checked the calendar on my phone.

No. No. No.

'Trixie,' I groaned. 'I've got to judge the cupcake contest!' I looked at my watch. 'I forgot all about it! And I should have been there ten minutes ago!'

Somehow, I drove across town without running anyone over, although a cat on the way came close to losing one of its nine lives. I parked the car, knocking over someone's rubbish bin, and ran into the hall. Here, I immediately noticed two things. The Cape Carson Scout Hall had been transformed into a culinary wonderland. Tables were beautifully decorated with cloths, silver display stands sparkled in the light, and a wide variety of cupcakes were displayed across the room in a blaze of colour.

The second thing I noticed were the several dozen heads that swivelled towards me as I came stumbling in the door. The buzz of conversation that had filled the hall immediately ceased. People stared. Even a baby in someone's arms abruptly stopped wailing. The scene was as frozen as the image of the apostles in Leonardo's Last Supper.

'Sorry,' I said, my voice echoing around the voluminous hall. 'Running a little late.'

Nobody spoke. A clock ticked on the wall. The whine of a car droned into the distance. The pregnant pause dragged on for the whole nine months—and then some—until Wanda Gibson let out a cry.

'Rosie!' she said as she clattered across the floor. 'Welcome! We were getting worried.'

The multitude of faces continued to stare. 'I wouldn't miss it for the world,' I declared loudly, my voice sounding horribly shrill in the silence. 'This is the event of the year!'

Still, no one spoke. Then the baby gave a single cry, which seemed to shatter the spell. People muttered among themselves. Two children chased each other among the legs of the adults. The normal flow of time resumed.

I crossed to the cupcake committee. 'I was held up,' I said. 'Or I would have been here earlier.'

'The crowd was getting restless,' the Reverend said. 'I feared another…*incident.*'

'There was talk—' Marlene began.

'We don't need to discuss that,' Wanda cut in.

'What?' I said. 'What talk?'

Marlene would not be stopped. 'People wanted to send out a search party to track you down.'

'Oh, yes,' I said, forcing a chuckle. 'A search party.'

No one else laughed. The image of a Cape Carson mob with burning torches raised, scouring the streets for me as they screamed *burn judge burn* flitted through my mind. I drove it away.

'Well, I'm here now,' I said, determined to forge ahead. 'Time to try some cupcakes.'

Wanda produced a clipboard with pages attached. I scanned the judging form. It contained several categories and a range of subcategories. Each section was a measure of one to ten, although there was provision for percentage points.

'Ah,' I said. 'The judging form.'

'You did read the manual?' Wanda said.

'Huh?'

'The Cupcake Judging manual,' Reverend Tyler said.

'Ah, yes. I went through it.' Surely *went through* was similar to reading. They were almost the same thing. 'I'm familiar with it. *Quite* familiar. So I'll get started.'

'We'll clear the hall first,' Wanda said.

'We don't need to clear the hall,' Marlene said. 'Section Seven, Subsection nine, Paragraph Three says that contestants may remain in the building.'

'The relevant word is *may*.'

Wanda clenched her teeth. 'Yes,' she said. '*May*.'

'Which can mean *may not*.'

'Or *may* as in *will*.'

'But not *may* as in *should* or *must*—'

Reverend Tyler began. 'Jesus said—'

'Jesus isn't on this committee,' Marlene said.

'But if he were—'

'Which he's not—'

Right now, Jesus's membership of the Cape Carson Cupcake Committee seemed a moot point. And I'd already had a long day. 'Everyone can leave...I mean...*will* leave while I judge,' I declared firmly. 'I need complete focus to decide the winner.'

This seemed to meet with Wanda's approval. She turned to the crowd with her booming voice. 'Everyone out!' she ordered. 'Judge Rosie requires full concentration to decide on a winner.'

I liked the sound of Judge Rosie. It made me think I should have my own television show. The occupants of the room grumbled. For a moment, I thought they might revolt, but then someone shuffled for the exit, and others followed.

Someone mentioned heading down to Sandy's Diner, and this was met with a rumble of agreement.

A woman who worked part-time at the bakery stopped at my elbow. 'Rosie,' she murmured. 'I found this under Table Four.'

It was a folded hundred-dollar note. The woman winked.

Oh, dear.

'Wanda,' I said. 'Please donate this to the Cape Carson Op Shop.'

'Absolutely.'

Soon, everyone was gone. I let out a long ragged breath. 'I think we only just survived,' I said, and she whined. 'I know. They're a weird mob.'

Surveying the judging sheet, I immediately realised there were so many categories and subcategories that I could be here all night. To make matters worse, there was an algebraic equation at the bottom of the page. All the numbers had to be slotted into it to make a final decision.

That's not happening. It had been over twenty years since I'd done algebra at high school, and I wasn't breaking that winning streak now! So, I had to invent my own system. Okay, that was easy enough. I'd try a cupcake from each table and then reach a decision.

Simple.

I crossed to the first table and started on a cupcake. It was a lovely thing. Pink and white with something that looked like gold leaf. I examined it more closely. Someone had created a map of the Cape Carson coastline on the top.

My goodness, I thought. *That's fantastic.*

After finishing that cake, I went to the next table and found that the creator had made a selection of cakes, all based around a musical theme. I peered closely at the top of the nearest one, wishing I had Carlos Windermere's eye-piece. Someone had written, in tiny letters, the words of a song: the National Anthem.

'Wow,' I thought.

It was a lovely cake too.

The following table proved just as inventive. Whoever had made these cakes had an interest in Australian wildflowers. Each cupcake had a perfect image of an Australian flower: Grevillea, Wattle, Bottlebrush, Kangaroo Paw.

Trixie whined and tilted her head as I chewed thoughtfully on one with the image of a Banksia on it.

'Sorry, girl,' I said. 'These are for people only.'

Turning to the judging sheet, I tried to take in the various columns: taste, texture, creativity, consistency...

Goodness, it was like trying to fill in the census. I expected to find a box asking what language I spoke at home.

'Hmm,' I said to Trixie. 'I don't need this. I'll decide at the end.'

As I glanced around at the rest of the tables, it was only now that I realised the task I had set myself.

Oh, dear. There were dozens more tables, and I'd committed to eating one cake from each. *How does the judge usually get through this?* I was already full. Dragging the manual from my bag, I turned to the section of judging and read:

A section measuring no larger than two centimetres square will be excised from the cupcake, divided into four, and eaten one piece at a time...

My eyes opened in horror as I lowered the manual.

'Oh no.'

20

'Rosie?' Nan said. 'Are you all right?'

'Peachy,' I groaned as I staggered in through the doorway. 'Although my stomach is about to explode.'

'Peppermint tea might help.'

'Please—and a stomach pump.'

Nan disappeared into the kitchen. My phone rang as I fell into the nearest lounge chair. It was Harry.

'How'd it all go?' he asked, sounding far too cheery for my liking.

'You *monster*...' I slurred. My face and hands were still sticky. Icing filled my hair. I was so high on sugar that I could have left the jeep and floated home. There were times as I stumbled from table to table that I thought I might die on the spot, and they'd discover me, dead on the floor with a cupcake jammed in my mouth. 'I hate you forever.'

'That bad?'

'Worse,' I said and explained what had happened.

Harry listened sympathetically. 'I should have warned you,' he said. 'I did that the first year too. Almost killed me. Should have read the instructions. Mind you, it's not a big problem if you don't have too many competitors.'

'How many did you have that first year?'

'Oh, it was challenging,' Harry said. 'Twelve.'

'Lord help me. I had twenty-eight.'

Silence followed. 'Okay,' he said. 'I'll leave you to it.'

He hung up as Nan returned to the living room brandishing a cup of peppermint tea and a plate.

'Look what I got you,' Nan said. 'A cupcake to cheer you up.'

Everything was a daze after that. It was the image of that cheerful pink and white cupcake with a smiley face on it that set me off.

I remember leaping from the lounge chair. The plate flying through the air. Trixie barking madly. Me stumbling to the bathroom. And the toilet bowl.

After a few minutes, Nan stuck her head around the doorway. 'Are you okay, Rosie?' she asked. 'Do you need a doctor?'

'I'm fine, Nan. I'll just crawl to bed.'

Although I didn't crawl, I did stagger badly. I lay down and didn't wake up again until the alarm went off the following day. My stomach was still not in good shape, and I felt like I'd been slapped around the head with a trout. Heading to the kitchen, I found Nan making tea for us.

'You're alive!' she said.

'Maybe,' I said. 'We'll see after I've had a cup of tea.'

'Oh, and these arrived for you.'

Nan pointed to a vase of flowers. I read the card that had accompanied them:

Hi Rosie,

I enjoyed our chat together.

Care to have dinner one night?

Colin.

I groaned. Just what I didn't need. Colin wasn't creepy, but he was old enough to be my father, and I had no interest in him romantically.

'Not from the man of your dreams?' Nan asked.

'Not even close.'

We grabbed our cups of tea and went to sit in the backyard. The day was cold, and the sky was a solid sheet of slate. A currawong cried mournfully in a faraway tree.

'So Roger Ableman won,' Nan said conversationally.

'Did he?' I said. 'Oh yes, I vaguely remember that. He must have found a good recipe in the library.'

I didn't even realise it was Roger who'd won. His cupcakes, decorated with pictures of clocks and timepieces, were quite different from anything produced by the other competitors. I told Nan about his theme.

'It sounds good to me, Rosie,' Nan said. 'Though don't be surprised if you cop some flak over it.'

'I'm sure it'll be fine.'

After finishing my tea, I headed inside to get ready. Despite having a big day ahead, I needed to do something straight away.

'Colin?' I said, ringing Katy Dark's ex-manager. 'Thanks so much for the flowers!'

'It's the least I could do. So is it yes to dinner?'

I hated to let the man down. 'I'm not really dating anyone at the moment,' I said. 'I'm trying to get used to being a single woman.'

Colin laughed gently. 'I don't give up easily,' he said. 'I'll still be around for a few days. I hope we can catch up.'

'I'm sure we'll see each other around.'

Thanking him again, I hung up and put a call through to Todd.

'Hey,' Todd said. 'It's my favourite reporter!'

'Even though I'm the only one you ever talk to, I'll take that as a compliment.' I paused. 'I was wondering if Chris had been released from jail yet.'

'No, Rosie. We don't release murder suspects from jail.'

'Can you give me any good news?'

He hesitated. 'Not news as such,' he said. 'I'm off to see Cameron Dark.'

'Why?'

'Just to ask him a few more questions.'

'And Chadek?'

'He's not talking,' Todd said. 'Actually, I'm a bit annoyed with you.'

'Why?'

'Chadek's clammed up tighter than a shell. He refuses to say anything, and I'm suspecting that single hint about the fake ring is all we're getting out of him.'

'Well,' I said defensively. 'That's not my fault.'

'You should leave police work up to the police.'

I felt like yelling at him. 'You wouldn't even know about the ring if it weren't for me,' I said. 'Chadek told me it was fake, not you. You'd still think the thing was worth millions if I hadn't spoken to him.'

Hanging up, I wondered why Chadek had given me the hint about the ring. He probably felt some gratitude because I saved his life. If I hadn't been there to call an ambulance, he would have died. Still, knowing the ring was fake didn't move us ahead a whole lot. I didn't know who stole it or when, and I didn't know who killed Katy.

Now that I thought about it, it seemed odd that she'd even brought it to Cape Carson. Why had she done that? So she could show it off to the locals? It was worth a fortune. Had she been wearing it much in recent months? I did a search of images online to see if any showed Katy wearing the ring. It only took me a few minutes to realise that she'd only worn it to big events. There was a movie preview in London. The release of a new fashion line in Brisbane. A perfume launch in Sydney.

My eyes narrowed on the picture.

What on Earth...?

I saved the link on my phone and quickly got ready to go out.

'You're off already?' Nan said. 'Not stopping for breakfast?'

'I never need to eat again. And if I see another cupcake....'

A few minutes later, I pulled up outside the Lighthouse Inn with Trixie at my side. A police car was already there. Instead of heading into the inn, Trixie and I rounded the building and made our way to the bungalow where Dorothy Stuart lived. A short, sharp knock brought her to the door.

'Rosie?' she said. 'What brings you—'

I waved the picture on my phone at her. 'Care to explain this?'

Her face froze. 'It's nothing.'

'Really?'

Dorothy reluctantly allowed me in, and I sat down on her couch. 'This is the launch in Sydney for the fragrance, *Love Lost*. There's Katy Dark and Cameron. And there's a bunch of people in the background. And look at who's standing in the crowd.'

Dorothy said nothing.

'It's you,' I said. 'Wow. What an incredible coincidence. You happened to be there.' I swiped through to another picture. 'And look here. Again. This time it's Brisbane. Now unless you want me to—'

'He's my father.'

I stopped. Staring in Dorothy's grey eyes, I suddenly saw what had been obvious this whole time. The truth literally had been staring me in the face. She had the same eyes. Same hairline. Even the same mouth. I should have realised it myself, but who would ever expect that a housemaid in Cape Carson would be the daughter of Cameron Dark?

Dorothy looked down. 'I'm not here to cause him harm,' she continued. 'I didn't hurt Katy. That's not why I came here. I tried sending him letters. He ignored them. I even tried speaking to him at one event, and he walked away.'

'How...' I started and then realised it was a silly question.

'My mother was young and impressionable. She met Cameron many years ago. They had a fling. When my mum told him she was pregnant, he wanted nothing to do with her. By then, she wasn't surprised. She'd already decided he was a conceited idiot. Mum raised me alone.' Dorothy stopped. 'But I always wondered about my dad. I wanted to speak to him. I wanted him to acknowledge me as a person. To acknowledge that I existed.'

'So that's why you came here.'

'This job became available, and I took it.'

That fitted with what I knew. But it wasn't the whole truth. 'Sheila said the previous girl was fired for stealing. That can't be a coincidence.'

Dorothy looked miserable. 'No,' she said. 'I came here one day and took something from a guest. Using a different name, I sent an email to Sheila, blaming the girl, and she was sacked. When I turned up the next day with my resume—'

'There was a job waiting for you.'

'I shouldn't have done it.' A tear rolled down Dorothy's cheek. 'But I wanted to know my father. I had nothing to do with Katy's death. I swear it!'

21

'So she did all that to speak to Cameron Dark,' Kim said.

We were watching the Cupcake parade with Nan, Dave, Amanda, and Tom. The entire town had come out to see the spectacle, and the footpaths were packed. People stood or sat on camping chairs and waved at the procession of slow-moving floats, decorated utes, and marching bands that trundled down Percy Street.

Sponsored by various organisations, the entertainers were dressed as different types of cupcakes. On both sides of the road, kids from the scouts and girl guides collected loose change from people for the local hospital.

'That's what Dorothy said,' I told Kim.

'Do you believe her?'

'I'm not sure.'

Nan, who was standing in front of me, turned around. 'Quiet you chatterboxes!' she said. 'Here comes the Post Office float.'

She always kept track of anything regarding the post office. Nan and my grandfather Frank had run the local post office for years before a middle-aged couple named Maureen and Ken took it over. The pair were on the back of a small truck dressed as cupcakes decorated in Express Post bags.

'Well,' I said. 'That's something you don't see every day.'

Nan nudged me. 'Don't be a smarty-pants.' Trixie barked. 'See, Trixie agrees with me.'

'I think they look great,' Amanda grumbled. 'I wanted a float. Tom said no.'

'Darling wife,' Tom said, patiently. 'I'll do many things to promote our business, but I refuse to dress like a cupcake.'

'Real men dress as cupcakes.'

'If you say so.'

'What about you, Dave?' I asked. 'Would you dress like a cupcake?'

Dave grinned. 'It's a tempting offer,' he said. 'But I'm waiting for the rock and roll festival.' He drove a hotted-up Valiant. 'I'll proudly drive my car down the road for charity.'

The rock and roll festival was still in the planning stages. Sandy from the diner was the brainchild behind the concept and had struggled to get it off the ground.

'Look!' Nan said, pointing. 'It's the library float!'

Kim waved wildly at her workmates.

The library always entered a float, and it never failed to

please. This year's float had a theme of a lady lying on a lounge reading a book. Beside her was an enormous bowl of cupcakes. Every so often, her hand would dip languidly into the bowl, and she'd take one out to eat. Or pretend to eat. I knew from my own experience that the human body could only take so many cupcakes before it revolted.

The last few floats trundled by, and the parade ended. Tom and Amanda decided to head into work to take advantage of the passing crowds. Nan and Dave opted to visit one of the smaller cafes in town while I went for a walk with Kim along the foreshore. At the beach, we removed our shoes to walk at the water's edge. Trixie, barking madly, chased seagulls up and down the beach.

'Now the conversation between Cameron and Dorothy makes more sense,' I said, thoughtfully.

'On the night of the murder?'

—can't do anything for you.

But I came all this way to see you.

Then you've wasted your time!

I'd already rung Todd with this information.

He'd confirmed the details with both Cameron and Sheila. I wasn't sure if Sheila would have criminal charges filed against Dorothy. She'd purposely framed someone for a crime, and they'd lost their job. If nothing else, I was sure Sheila wouldn't be too happy.

After finishing our walk along the beach, I told Kim I had another lead to follow up. The one person we hadn't spoken to was Jason. Although he hadn't stayed at the inn overnight, Jason may have seen something suspicious.

'I'll come with you,' Kim offered.

'Are you sure?'

'Absolutely. I want to help if it will lead to finding the real killer.'

Whereas I already had Jason's address, I didn't have a phone number. He lived in Barkly, a tiny town five kilometres north of Cape Carson. Soon we were driving away from the coast and through the bush surrounding the town. Kim opened the passenger window so Trixie could gaze out. The wind tore past her head, causing her ears to flap about wildly.

We both laughed.

'I'm glad my ears don't do that,' Kim said, shuddering. 'I once went out with a guy who had big ears.'

'It didn't work out?'

'I couldn't stop looking at his ears. It was like having dinner with an alien from Doctor Who.'

We soon reached Barkly, a place that was little more than a one-horse town, with a few residential streets and a single row of shops. Jason's home was an old fibro place encircled by a vast vegetable garden.

'Hey,' Jason said, answering our knock at the door as the

wailing of a baby emanated from the interior. 'It's the media!'

'Rosie Ryan,' I said. 'And my friend Kim.' I explained we wanted to ask a few questions. 'Do you mind?'

'As long as you don't mind putting up with little Petey,' he said. 'He's screaming the place down.'

The living room beyond was a minefield of plastic toys. We manoeuvred around these to sit around an old, laminated kitchen table. Glancing around, I saw the rest of the house had a similar theme: 1950's Australian. There were even ceramic flying ducks on the lounge room wall.

Jason sat Petey on the floor and Trixie obligingly allowed herself to be patted by the infant. Petey stopped crying.

Good girl, I thought.

'We were hoping to ask you about the other night,' Kim began.

'No worries,' Jason said. 'The cops didn't want to ask me anything.'

'Really?' I said. 'They didn't speak to you?'

'One of them asked what time I left. He wasn't interested when I said I left straight after dinner. Besides, they arrested that guy pretty quick smart.'

'Was there anything unusual that evening?'

'Not at dinner. I was in the kitchen prepping with Dorothy. She's good, that girl. Fast and efficient.' He picked up Petey, bouncing him on his knee. 'No, it was before dinner when I saw the fireworks happen.'

'What do you mean?'

'It was between Katy Dark and that other guy. The older bloke.'

'Colin Wood? Her ex-manager?'

'That's him. Katy had gone out the back to have a quiet moment. There's an old bench behind the kitchen. She was out there taking a breather when he cornered her. I was in the kitchen, and the window was open, so I could hear what was going on.'

'What were they saying?' Kim asked.

'The old guy said that Katy owed him. He'd spent a lot of money over the years managing her and hadn't been paid back.'

'How did she react?' I asked.

'She was furious. I think it would have turned into a screaming match, except they knew people were around. There was one thing Colin said that I heard loud and clear: *You're going to pay for what you've done.*'

These words reverberated in my mind.

You're going to pay for what you've done.

No denying it, that was ominous. Jason had little more to add, so we thanked him and returned to the car. I told Kim I wanted to head back to the Lighthouse Inn to speak to Colin. Kim said she'd come with me.

At the inn, Kim and I headed through the front door just as the grandfather clock chimed upstairs. 'Three o'clock already,' I said, glancing at my watch.

Sheila came barrelling out from the back room. 'Rosie!' she exclaimed. 'And Kim! So glad you're here. All those horrible reporters are finally gone. Oh, I don't include you in that, Rosie. You're local, and I know your Nan. But I'll be so relieved when everything returns to normal—'

'Are any of the guests in?' I asked.

'Only Colin and Cameron.'

We thanked her, went upstairs, and I knocked politely on Colin's door. He flung it open and smiled brightly when he saw it was me. 'Rosie!' he said. His smile faltered. 'And Kim.'

'And Trixie,' I said. 'Can we talk?'

'Of course.'

We entered. 'We'd like to chat about a conversation you had with Katy before she died.'

'Yes?'

I wasn't sure how to broach the subject. 'It's just that...well...'

'Did you threaten Katy Dark?' Kim blurted.

'*What?*' Colin said, alarmed.

I shot Kim a sideways glance before forging on. 'Colin. We've been told you and Katy argued on the day she died. You apparently said *You're going to pay for what you've done*. Is that true?'

'Oh *that*,' Colin said, chuckling as his alarm turned to relief. 'It was nothing. Just a business disagreement. I don't know who's been telling tales out of school, but, yes, we argued. We always did. Goodness, one time, Katy hit me with a saucepan. We were always saying the most dreadful things to each other.' He sobered. 'Mind you, there was a lot of love there too. We cared for each other.'

'She did fire you as her manager,' I pointed out.

Colin shrugged. 'Katy married Cameron,' he said. 'He could do much the same job as me, and he'd do it for free. Mind you, Cameron's no manager. He couldn't manage a chook raffle. And I'm not saying the breakup didn't hurt me. It did. But this was business, and business is always like that.'

Strangely, Colin's explanation seemed reasonable. I knew from experience that people in the entertainment industry could be working together while simultaneously suing each other. They created a barrier with business firmly on one side and personal relationships on the other.

Thanking Colin, we were about to leave when he asked if he could have a quiet word. Kim gave me a look before heading out to the hallway to wait.

'Rosie,' he said. 'I'm hoping to take you up on that offer of a get-together.'

I hadn't suggested a meeting, although I did owe him a

coffee.

He continued. 'I don't know anyone in this area, and it would be lovely to get out.'

'There are some nice spots up and down the coast—'

'Maybe we could do dinner?' Colin suggested. 'Please? It would make my day.'

I hesitated. Although I didn't want to give Colin the wrong impression, he was a stranger to this area, and it had been a tough few days for everyone. 'That would be great,' I said. 'I never say no to food.'

His face brightened. 'Where would you suggest?'

'Casual or upmarket?'

'Anything's fine.'

Laughing, I told him I hoped he didn't mind burgers and suggested we meet at Sandy's. We agreed to meet at six. Saying goodbye, I headed downstairs with Kim and told her about dinner with Colin.

'Well,' she said. 'You could do worse.'

'Relax. He's not my type.'

We were just about to leave when Sheila appeared at the reception desk and waved us over.

'I'm glad you girls are still here,' she said. 'There's something I wanted to mention, and it's been playing on my mind.' The woman wrung her hands together. 'I didn't bring it up before because I didn't want to cause any more trouble. And it may mean nothing.'

I was getting a little impatient. 'What is it, Sheila?'

'After everyone arrived on that first night, I was pottering about the place, tidying up. Getting everything ready. I was worried because we had such famous people staying here. I wanted everything to be just right. People can be so nasty sometimes when they write online reviews—'

'Sheila!'

'Oh, my mouth runs on sometimes. Have you noticed? Anyway, Katy and Cameron were in the garden together. They were having a discussion, and some very unpleasant things were being said. She said he had better watch out because she knew what he'd done, and he said something about her ending up in a box.'

Kim and I exchanged glances. 'Wow,' Kim said. 'That *does* sound nasty.'

'Why didn't you mention this before, Sheila?' I asked.

'I was hoping this whole thing would just blow over—and the police had already arrested Chris Dawson. It seemed like an open and shut case.'

I told Sheila I had to confront Cameron with this, but I promised I wouldn't bring her name into it. Kim and I trooped back upstairs to Cameron's room. I was just about to knock when his door opened.

'Oh,' he said. 'Hello, ladies.'

'Do you have a moment?'

'Just one. I need to go for a drive to clear my head. And Garry needs a walk. I haven't been looking after him properly.'

We peered into the room. Garry was sitting dejected on the bed. Trixie gave a happy whine and pushed past him into the room. Seizing the opportunity, I told Cameron I wanted to talk about a conversation that someone had overheard. I was halfway through relating it when he gave a bitter laugh.

'Oh,' he said. 'That.' He spoke theatrically. '*You'd better watch your step, otherwise you'll end up in a box!*'

Kim and I both stared at him.

'We were doing lines,' he said. 'From *The President's Robot*. Katy and I were practicing for her upcoming movie.' His face fell. 'I mean…it was going to be her movie.'

'I'm sorry,' I said.

He shook himself. 'Anyway,' he said. 'I don't know why you're asking me this. You know I spent the night with Cindy. I couldn't have killed my wife. And Chris has been caught. Hasn't he confessed to her murder?'

'No,' Kim said defiantly. 'And I believe he's innocent.'

Cameron looked surprised but then shrugged. 'You could be right,' he said. 'I was shocked when Chris was arrested. I never envisioned him as a killer.'

'So who do you suspect?' I asked.

'The same person I've always suspected: Charlotte. She was

far too clingy for my liking. And she had a strange look in her eye. More than once, I noticed her staring at Katy—no, *glaring* at Katy as if she hated her.'

'Have you seen Charlotte around?'

'She's left the inn.'

'Really? The police asked that no one leave the area.'

'She only lives an hour away.' He frowned. 'Personally, I'm glad she's gone.'

I thought back to the *C* written beside Katy's body. It seemed unlikely that Charlotte could have known about the relationship between Chris and Katy.

Still, she could have taken the phone, stolen the ring, and murdered Katy. I hadn't felt comfortable around her from the moment she arrived.

Cameron was clearly in a hurry to get moving. He picked up Garry and I thanked him for his time.

'That's okay,' he said. 'But let me give you some free advice: be careful around that woman. She's downright odd.'

'Thanks,' I said. 'I'll watch my step.'

22

'Ah-ha!' Colin said. 'The woman with the wonderful bag!'

I laughed. 'I know what you mean,' I said. 'It's so big I can fit a kangaroo in there.'

Sandy's Diner was packed with people, so I was glad I'd booked a table earlier. Colin and I were nestled towards the back in a booth. There was a family on one side of us and a bunch of teenagers on the other. The music reverberating through the loudspeakers was Roy Orbison. The place was pumping.

'Are all these people local?' Colin asked.

'It's about fifty-fifty,' I said, gazing around. 'A lot have come for the festival.'

Colin shook his head in admiration. 'Who would ever think that something like a Cupcake Festival would be such a draw-card?'

Sandy arrowed over with menus. 'Hey, people,' she said. 'The lasagne's on special tonight. We also have a burger, chips, and dessert combo.'

'That sounds good to me,' Colin said, adding extra bacon and cheese to his burger.

'I'll have the same,' I said. 'It's been a tough day.'

Sandy jotted down our order and hurried off to the kitchen.

'Have you made any headway in your investigation?' Colin asked as our drinks arrived.

'It's not really an investigation. My grandmother has been friends with Sheila for a long time. I'm just trying to help out.'

'And there's no Mister Ryan in your life?'

I laughed. 'There *was* a Mister Ryan. He went gallivanting about with a younger woman. Now there's just me.'

'His loss!'

'I agree!'

We laughed. By the time our food appeared, I felt a lot more relaxed. Colin chatted about being Katy's manager and working in the industry while I spoke about my years as an entertainment reporter. He nodded to my blouse.

'That's a lovely outfit,' he said. 'Although you've had a little accident.'

I glanced down. True to form, I'd dribbled sauce from my burger down my top. Silently cursing, I dabbed most of it away. 'Don't mind me,' I said. 'I'm always dropping food on myself, so I can snack later.'

'Might need a bit more water on that,' he advised.

'True.'

In the bathroom, I was diluting the stain when my phone rang.

'Hey Todd,' I said.

'Having a good night?'

There was something in the way he said it that made me pause. 'Not bad,' I said. 'Why do you ask?'

'I just took Rocko for a walk,' he said airily. 'I happened to notice you in Sandy's with Colin.'

'We're just friends,' I said. 'Well, not even that. Colin asked me to dinner.'

'I see.'

'*We're* supposed to be going to dinner,' I said pointedly.

'I know.'

'Oh,' I said, remembering. 'By the way, I think you should take another look at Charlotte.' I explained what Cameron had told us. 'She always struck me as a bit odd too.'

'She did seem intense,' Todd admitted. 'Although, do I need to remind you—'

'That you've already arrested someone? No.'

I wished him a good night and hung up.

That man!

My phone rang again: Kim.

'Hey you,' Kim said, sounding out of breath. 'How's the date going?'

'It's not a date. And you're panting. Are you out running?'

'I just happened to jog by the diner and noticed Colin in there alone.'

Kim was a keen jogger and had twice won the Cape Carson Marathon. 'He's sitting by himself because people keep ringing me!' I said. 'Chat later!'

After washing my hands, I returned to the table where I mentioned my call with Todd.

Colin rubbed his chin thoughtfully. 'I feel rather guilty about recommending Chris,' he said. 'I put out the feelers some time ago to find an author who could work with Katy. I had no idea it would lead to this.'

Sandy's Diner was noisier than ever. We finished our meal as more people poured in the door, so I suggested calling it a night. He agreed. Outside the restaurant, he asked if we could go out again sometime while he was in town.

'I don't really know this part of the coast,' he said. 'It would be lovely to go for a scenic tour.'

I hesitated. Then—why not? 'That would be fine,' I said. 'I'll check my calendar, and we can take a drive.'

'Wonderful.'

Returning to my jeep, I'd just climbed in behind the wheel when my phone buzzed. I looked down.

Wow, I thought. *That's lucky.*

An email had arrived from Charlotte. She didn't have my

phone number, so she'd used the office email address. The message read:

Hi Rosie,

I have information to share about Katy's death that you might find interesting. Can you come to my place tomorrow morning at 9.00?

27 Shivers Lane, Bombatta.

Thanks,

Charlotte.

Great. This could lead to something. Charlotte might have remembered something from the night of Katy's death. I started the engine and drove home. Pulling into the driveway, I felt concerned. Charlotte could know something, or she could be the killer. She could be drawing me into a trap.

I'd better be careful.

'Have a nice night?' Nan asked as I entered. She was still working on the jigsaw puzzle at the kitchen table.

Trixie came bounding down the hallway, and I patted her. 'It was fine,' I said, peering at the puzzle. 'You've really made some headway.'

'It's not easy. After all…'

'Let me guess. Rome wasn't built in a day?'

'You've heard that before?'

'Only about a million times.'

I told her that Colin seemed like a nice man, but not my

type. 'We're going for a drive in a few days.'

'And you still think that fella, Chris, isn't the killer?'

Over the next few minutes, I related what we'd discovered so far. Nan asked a few questions here and there until she finally shook her head.

'It's like these puzzles,' she said. 'It's the missing pieces. They seem so obvious once they're in place, but when you're looking at the gap, it's just a void. It's something that's missing that you know should be there—and it's not.'

Deep in thought, I stared down at the image. Nan was right. There'd been a nagging sensation in my gut from the time Katy was murdered. Something didn't make sense.

What am I missing?

23

The countryside was green and lush as I drove north from Cape Carson to Bombatta. There wasn't a cloud in the sky. Once I'd left town, I pulled over on the crest of a hill and got out to take in the view. The scene I looked down on took my breath away.

There was the vast sky, silent and clear.

Beneath it lay rolling fields that disappeared into the distance. Cows and sheep dotted the green hills. I felt small when I looked out as if I were a tiny speck of dust. Above lay the universe: below, solid Earth.

'Kind of puts everything into perspective,' I said, stroking Trixie's neck. She gave a bark and nestled her head against my leg. 'You're an old softie. What would I do without you, girl?'

We climbed back into the car and continued on. Half an hour later, we were driving through a vast patch of bushland. I'd been to Bombatta before—or more accurately, I'd been through Bombatta. It was another one of those thousands of towns that dot the Australian landscape, places you zoom through because you're going somewhere else.

A speed sign telling me to slow down was immediately followed by a town sign that read Bombatta. There was no town, only an intersection. There weren't even houses on each corner. Just bush on three sides and a ramshackle cottage on the fourth. The map on my phone steered me left down a dirt road.

Here and there, like ritualistic totems, sat letterboxes on posts, with driveways behind them that vanished into the bush. Putting the window down, I breathed in the scent of eucalyptus, wattles, and tea trees.

This is a perfect day.

Finally, I reached the euphemistically named *Shivers Lane*, which turned out to be another dusty, potholed road. I turned down it, following for another ten minutes as the bush closed in on both sides and the road grew worse. I was grateful for my jeep.

Goodness. Where is this woman's place?

Then a clearing appeared on my right, and I spotted a small lawn with a vegetable garden and a two-storey timber and mud-brick house beyond. A sloping timber awning shaded the verandah. On one side sat a chicken coop. On the other was a car I recognised as Charlotte's, nestled beneath a faded red and blue sail. Behind it, in the gloom, sat another vehicle smothered under a tarp.

This wasn't what I expected. I liked it, though, as rough and ready places like this had their own charm. Oddly, people seeking solitude would pay good money to live in such a place. As I got out of the jeep, the house's front screen door clattered open, and Charlotte appeared.

'Rosie,' she said. 'Glad you could make it.'

'Thanks for inviting me.'

Her eyes narrowed on Trixie. 'Would you mind if your pooch stayed in your car?' she said. 'I'm allergic to dogs.'

She hadn't mentioned it while we were at the Lighthouse Inn. 'I didn't know that.'

'I can usually keep it under control with antihistamines, but I'm out at the moment.'

Leaving Trixie in the car, I cracked open the windows to allow air in. She gave a tiny whine as I closed the door. I told her I wouldn't be long and crossed to the house. Charlotte was staring at me with an odd look on her face. Something between a frown and a grin.

'Come in,' she said. 'I'll make us tea.'

The building had an earthy smell, but it was more than that. It was almost herbal. Knowing how odd Charlotte had seemed, I wondered if she were cooking with herbs or smoking them.

The hallway was dark after the bright day outside. Blinking

to accustom my eyes to the gloom, I saw dozens of framed pictures lining the walls.

I started. 'These pictures are all from....'

'Horseshoe Farm.'

The hall opened onto a living room. Over the fireplace hung a framed picture of Cameron Dark when he was younger. Although he was handsome now, he'd been an absolute stud back then, almost like a young Brad Pitt. I wasn't in the mood for admiring hot men, however, as a sense of disquiet had begun to stew in my belly.

I don't like the feel of this.

Other framed pictures lined the living room. Most appeared to be behind-the-scenes shots from a movie. I gazed more closely at one. 'Is that you?' I asked.

Charlotte nodded. 'I worked on the movie, Hilldale,' she said. 'It was Cameron's second film. That's where I first met him.'

'Okay.' The odd feeling in my gut intensified. 'You didn't mention that before.'

'I thought it best not to. People don't understand.'

'What don't they understand?'

But Charlotte had disappeared into the kitchen. What filled the silence was a memory of when we'd first met Katy Dark. *Aren't you worried about stalkers?* That's what Charlotte had said to her.

My eyes moved across the room. Charlotte had known Cameron Dark during the filming of Hilldale. She was more than a fan. Her goal in entering the contest wasn't to meet Katy; she wanted to see Cameron again. Then there were all those threatening letters. A stalker *could* have killed Katy Dark. They could have also hatched some elaborate scheme to frame Chris. Whatever happened to Katy wasn't random: it was planned.

A framed photo sat next to a well-worn armchair. From here, Charlotte sat and watched television. Maybe even ate her meals. I picked up the picture. The photo was a faded image of Cameron and Charlotte together. Cameron was looking off-shot as if he had somewhere to go, but Charlotte looked immensely pleased. Like a delirious teenager.

'There's an enduring connection between Cameron and me,' Charlotte said. 'No one can take that away.'

Turning, I saw two things at once.

The first was that Charlotte hadn't been making tea. The second was that she'd gone off to retrieve a rifle, and it was aimed directly at me.

'Oh,' I said, my voice high. 'That's a very nice rifle you've got.'

'It belonged to my father. He used to hunt rabbits with it.'

That line from the Elmer Fudd cartoons ran through my head.

Be vewy, vewy quiet. I'm hunting wabbits!

'Oh yes,' I said, as my heart slammed hard in my chest. 'Those troublesome rabbits. Never liked them myself.' Glancing sideways, I tried to work out if I could make a break for the front door. I couldn't; I wouldn't get five feet. 'Is there any particular reason why you've got your gun pointed at me?'

Charlotte went slack-jawed, but her eyes were dark. 'Because Cameron loves me,' she said. 'Not you.'

'I...well...yes, obviously he loves you. I don't think he likes me much. He finds me a pain. Most people do. Just ask my friends.'

'But I saw how he looked at you,' she said. 'And there you were, batting your eyelashes at him.'

'Really? That's a condition I have: eyelash dystopia—'

Her eyes narrowed on the frame in my hand. 'What are you holding?' she demanded. 'Put it down!'

'This picture?' I stepped nearer. 'It's a beautiful photo of you and Cameron together. You're a lovely looking couple.'

'Put it down!'

I moved another step closer. 'Of course,' I said. 'This must be very precious to you—'

'Put it down!'

Nodding reassuringly, I went to sit it down on the coffee table. Instead, I swung the picture about, swatting the rifle. *Bang!* It went off, blowing a hole in a lampshade. I charged at Charlotte, elbowing her in the face and knocking the gun from her hand.

It clattered to the floor, and we both scrambled for it.

'He's mine!' Charlotte snarled. 'Mine!'

'You can have him!'

Charlotte reached the rifle first. As she picked it up, I saw there was no way I could wrestle it from her in time, so I gave her a hard shove and sent her sprawling into the hallway. If I tried to scramble over her to the front door, Charlotte would easily shoot me in the back, so I raced in the opposite direction. Spying a set of stairs leading upwards, I ran up to the next floor. Here I was faced by another hallway where doors led from both sides. Racing to the first door, I tried it.

Locked!

I ran to the next.

Locked!

The sound of feet thudding up the stairs echoed through the house.

Charlotte screamed. 'You'll be sorry you ever laid eyes on Cameron!'

I'm already sorry!

I tried the next door.

Locked!

I desperately threw myself at the last door on the right, and it flew open. I scanned the room: bed, wardrobe, dressing table, chair. Dragging the dressing table in front of the door, I raced to the window.

Painted shut!

Charlotte let out another scream as she threw herself against the door. The door shook, pushing the dressing table out a few inches. I was no match against a woman with a gun. Grabbing up the chair, I swung it at the glass.

Smash!

I broke away the jagged pieces and clattered onto the sloping timber awning. It was slippery up here, but I could climb down if I was careful. Then—

My phone rang.

I dragged it from my bag.

'Help!' I screamed. *'Help me—'*

It took a moment to understand the voice at the other end.

'—want to complain about the results,' the woman said. 'My sugar-free cupcakes would have had a far better chance of winning—'

I tried to hang up. Instead, my fingers slipped, I dropped my phone, and it went clattering into the gutter. The dressing table toppled over as Charlotte forced her way into the room. Trying to edge down the awning, my feet slipped from under me, and I landed on my bottom.

Yelling, I slid down the awning, found myself momentarily airborne, hit the ground, somehow landing on my feet. My forward momentum propelled me into the dirt. I raced around the house as another shot rang out. I got to my jeep, pulled open the door, and started the engine.

Trixie whined as I slammed my foot on the accelerator and screamed up the dirt track away from the house.

'It's okay, girl,' I said, swallowing. 'Just another day on the job.'

24

'We found your phone,' Todd said. 'But there's no sign of Charlotte.'

It had been a long day. After finding a friendly farmer who lived on the main road, I'd rung the police, and they'd turned up with an ambulance.

The police had conducted an exhaustive search of Charlotte's property while the ambulance officers examined me. Fortunately, all I'd suffered were cuts and bruises.

Now Todd and I were sitting in his police vehicle outside Charlotte's house.

'That doesn't worry me,' I replied. 'The further she is away from me, the better.'

Constable Turner left the house and came over. 'That's pretty amazing in there,' he said to us. 'Every room is full of pictures of that actor Cameron Dark. A lot she drew herself, and believe me, she's no artist.' He shook his head. 'And then there's one room that makes no sense at all.'

'What's in it?' Todd asked.

'Magazines. Thousands of copies of the same magazine.'

'Let me make a guess,' I said. 'They're all the same issue of Women's Life. That explains how she won the contest. She submitted thousands of entries.'

The constable went back inside.

'That's love for you,' I said.

'That's not love, Rosie,' Todd said. 'That's obsession. It also explains the threatening letters to Katy.'

'So you think Charlotte sent them?'

'You don't think so?'

I sighed. 'I'm not sure. The most recent letters all looked like they'd been written by someone using their non-dominant hand, and the most recent one was a different type of paper.' I stared at the ramshackle house. 'She could have murdered Katy, but did Charlotte have the know-how or the contacts to have a replica ring made? And is Katy's death and the theft of the ring even connected?'

'We *have* already arrested someone for Katy's murder,' Todd reminded me.

I groaned. 'I know. You've aimed for the lowest hanging fruit.'

'We have to follow where the evidence takes us.' He stopped. 'Though there is something you may be interested in.'

'And that is?'

'Chadek's out of the hospital.'

'Already? The guy was shot.'

Todd shrugged. 'He's tough. I'll give him that. I think he may have felt safer out of the hospital than in.'

My phone beeped. I had a message from George.

Are we still on for tonight?

I'd forgotten all about going to dinner with him. Right now, I felt like collapsing on the lounge and binging some mindless television. Still, I didn't want to cancel; he might take it as an insult, and I didn't want that. George was Amanda's dad, and there was no reason to get him offside.

I texted back.

Sure.

Thanking Todd, I headed for my car where Trixie was impatiently waiting. 'Hey girl,' I said. 'Exciting times.'

She barked.

'Yeah. I know what you mean. Some excitement we can do without.'

I headed back to the office to update Harry. The paper was going to print today. It was mid-afternoon and there was always a frantic rush to get everything done, but today everything seemed particularly chaotic.

Harry was at his desk, typing furiously. 'Rosie!' he barked. 'Is your story about Katy's murder ready yet?'

'Almost.'

'Then get onto it. Casey's Supermarket booked a double-page ad for this edition. As well as your story, we need two pages of filler.'

Because of how printing worked, we couldn't simply add two pages. We needed a multiple of four.

'Right onto it,' I said.

Doris gave me a look as I passed her desk.

'—an illegal ingredient?' she was saying. 'What was the ingredient? Sugar? No, I'm sure that doesn't count—'

Down the corridor, Ellie glanced up from her computer. 'You heard about the double-page spread?'

'Did they supply artwork?'

'Yes, but I've got to resize the fonts. They've got too many pictures and not enough text.'

Reaching my office, I had to stifle a laugh as I saw Jay literally taking two calls at once.

'Yes,' he was saying. 'We'll come to see you tomorrow...yes, it's too late for this week's edition...and, yes, I know ping pong is important.' He hung up on that call and turned to the mobile in his hand. 'Mrs Clifton, we'll get back to you on that story about pools.'

'Busy day?' I asked.

Jay turned to me in relief as he put down the phone. 'Rosie! So glad you're here. I'm doing a piece on the council chambers redevelopment. Harry's working on something and—'

'Relax.' I sat at my computer and opened a new file. 'Let me weave some magic.'

Everything that had happened over the last few days ran through my mind. Most of the story was written. That would do for the front page. I also had a lot of background material I could use as filler for the interior. My fingers flew over the keyboard.

An hour later, I finally sat back. 'Okay,' I said. 'I've got something.'

I sent it to Harry to format.

After a moment, a holler came from his office. 'Thanks!'

I called back. 'You're welcome!'

Over the next few minutes, I perused the other stories for this week's edition. Harry had done a sterling job handling the lion's share of the writing. Jay had written some good copy too. Lots of stuff about the cupcake competitors. Plenty of photos of the parade. My story was in there about the brawl. Then—

I glowered. 'Do we really need that headline?'

'Huh?' Jay said.

'*Controversial Result at Cupcake Final*,' I read. 'It sounds like I chose the wrong winner.'

'Harry wrote that.'

I marched into Harry's office. 'Really?' I said. 'Controversial result?'

'It's eye-catching.' Harry glanced up from his computer.

'Besides, not everyone agrees with your result.'

'Like who?'

'Like half the town.'

'What?'

Laughing, Harry sat back in his chair. 'Rosie, everyone's got their own opinion about everything. You've never noticed that the whole town comes down on me like a ton of bricks whenever I choose the winner?'

'Um...'

'That's right. There's always controversy about who wins. Get used to it. And if it means anything, I went to the exhibit and tried one of Roger's cupcakes. It was good.' He reflected. 'Maybe not as good as Marlene's, but she does make sweets for a living.'

I grumbled. 'I give up.'

'Good. Now give me another five hundred words about the history of the Cape Carson Lighthouse. I still have a quarter page to fill.'

25

I walked out of the Gazette office feeling tired but satisfied. The newspaper was going to press. The front page was crowded with big news stories about the festival and the murder of Katy Dark. My work for the day was done.

Now all I had to deal with was my very complicated social life. I was having dinner with George and felt more than a little apprehensive. Trixie could obviously sense how I was feeling. She whined as we got into my jeep, and I started the engine.

'Lucky girl,' I said, ruffling her neck. 'You're single. Men are more trouble than they're worth.'

Trixie barked.

'Oh, all right,' I relented. 'They're not all bad. You might find a special floppy-eared friend one day.'

Driving home, I found the entire family—Nan, Dave, Amanda, and Tom—in the kitchen, working on the jigsaw puzzle.

'Roped in more victims?' I said to Nan.

'Well, you know, Rome wasn't—'

'I know. I know.'

I headed to my bedroom to get changed. As I struggled to work out what to wear, there was a knock at the door, and Amanda peeked in.

'Can we talk?' she asked.

'Sure.' I stood before my mirror, trying to tame my hair into something other than a bird's nest. 'I should have gone to the hairdresser.'

Amanda settled onto the bed and gazed up at me. 'Really? For dinner with Dad?'

I glanced at her in the mirror. 'Are you still annoyed with your father?'

'Sure. Aren't you?'

'Absolutely.'

'Then why are you going out with him?'

'It's just dinner. We're not getting remarried.'

'I should hope not.'

I sat beside her. 'Don't start thinking that I've forgotten what happened,' I said. There were things you could never forget. 'But I saw your dad in town the other day, and he looked a little down.'

'I'm not against you cheering him up. I still love him.'

'Of course, you love him! He's your dad!'

Amanda looked away before continuing. 'I think he and

Blossom have broken up.'

I gazed at her. 'Really?' I said. 'That's unexpected.'

'Can't you at least look pleased?'

'Honey, I was furious with your dad for a long time. Then I realised the only person I was hurting was me. He was getting on with his life while I was stewing like an old sock in a pile of washing.'

'Hmm,' Amanda said. 'And at least you've got Todd.'

I laughed, maybe too loudly. 'We're just friends.'

'Sure you are.'

I drew Amanda close. 'Nothing's happening between Todd and me.'

'Then maybe something should.'

I wriggled on my shoes and somehow wrestled my hair under control. 'Our relationship is purely professional. And I'm going to dinner with your father to have a nice time. I'm relaxed. You need to relax too.'

'Really? You seem kind of tense.'

'What makes you say that?'

'Maybe it's the mismatched shoes.'

I glanced down at my fashion faux pas. 'This is the latest style,' I said. 'Everyone's doing it.'

'Let them.' Amanda made me sit while she swapped them around. 'Go with traditional.'

'Today's kids have no sense of style.'

We stared at each other—and burst out laughing.

A few minutes later, I was walking in the door of Super Thai, my eyes scanning the interior for George. He wasn't easy to spot. The lighting in the place was subdued. Probably to hide the grime. Then I spotted the top of a familiar head. *There he is.* My ex-husband had positioned himself at a table near the window. He gave me a peck on the cheek, and I sat down opposite. I gave him a quick up and down. He'd ironed a shirt and put on new jeans. He'd also shaved and smelt good. And what was that cologne? CK One? I wasn't sure if he'd done all this for me or if he'd decided to clean up his act.

After checking the menu, we ordered food and drinks.

'So what's been happening with you?' he asked. 'I heard you made quite a splash at the judging.'

I told him everything that had occurred over the last few days, including the contest and the mystery surrounding Katy Dark. Looking more closely, it struck me that George had put on more weight than I thought. Too many pizzas, maybe. It always beat me how Blossom could stand living in the same house as George and Nico.

I'd driven by a few times and noticed fruit trees had been planted around the garden. Maybe that was her attempt to make the place liveable.

Our drinks and food arrived. By now, I realised that George was strangely quiet. 'So, how are things going with you?' I asked. 'And Blossom? And Nico?'

'Well, you know Nico. He needs to focus more on work and less on partying.'

'And Blossom?'

George gave a bitter laugh. 'A few ups and downs,' he said. 'Blossom is still away.'

'Okay. The harmonic...er, thing? How long is that for?'

'I'm not sure.'

Really? That didn't sound like the foundation of a good relationship: *my partner is away, and I have no idea when she's returning.*

'Actually,' George continued, 'I'm not sure if she's coming back.'

'Oh,' I said quietly. 'So it's a breakup?'

He shrugged. It was hard to know what to say. *I'm sorry to hear that* wasn't true. I wasn't pleased to hear it. Nor was I displeased.

'I suppose that makes you happy,' he said.

'Not at all.'

He talked about his plumbing business in Cape Carson. He and Nico were working on a block of villa units at the back of town. I stared out the window while he spoke, my gaze settling on the lighthouse. Katy Dark had died up there, and her killer was still loose. Who could it be? At that exact instant, Kim went running past. She looked hot and exhausted. Kim exercised a lot when she was stressed.

She must be worried about Chris.

'...if it's possible,' George was saying.

'Huh?'

He frowned. 'I was saying that maybe things could go back to how they were,' he said. 'Well, maybe not exactly how they were—'

I stared at him.

Is he really suggesting we get back together?

'Yes, that would be hard,' I said, unable to keep the bitterness from my voice. 'There's been a lot of water under the bridge.'

'We all make mistakes.'

'Though some mistakes are bigger than others. And what about Blossom?'

'She can look after herself.'

'Really?' I'd been feeling tired until this moment. Now my vision became crystal clear as if I were seeing George for the first time. 'Blossom can look after herself?'

'I'm just saying—'

'Like I was left to look after myself? The only person who seems to continually come out on top in all this is you, George. First, you want to rumba with your secretary, and you do. Then you decide you'd like to come back to Cape Carson, and you do that too. Then you decide you might like to take the old grey mare for one last gallop.' I stopped. 'Don't you think that's how it sounds?'

George reddened. 'I'm sorry you feel like that,' he said. 'Don't you think everyone needs to follow their heart?'

Follow their—?

'That sounds like something Blossom would say,' I said, then stared down at my meal. I felt sick, and it wasn't from the lousy food. 'I've had enough.'

Although George tried to say something more, I stood and scooped up my handbag. It tipped upside down, and the contents from the multitude of pockets sprayed onto the floor. I untidily pushed everything back in and headed for the door.

After hastily paying the bill, George caught up with me on the footpath and grabbed my arm. 'Rosie,' he said. 'It's not like that.'

'Really?' The night was as chilly as the inside of a freezer, but my face was burning. 'It certainly sounds like that. I don't see how—'

A figure appeared from the darkness. 'Rosie!' a voice said in surprise. 'Is everything all right!'

Colin Wood stepped forward, his eyes on George's arm. My ex-husband released me.

'Everything's fine,' George said flatly.

'Hello Colin,' I said. 'Everything's great.' Deciding I couldn't leave it at that, I introduced him to George.

Colin's face was unreadable. 'Nice to meet you.'

'Ditto.'

'Anyway,' I said firmly to George. 'I'll be seeing you.'

'Yeah, sure.'

George departed without another word and disappeared into the darkness. Colin's eyes met mine.

'Hope I didn't interrupt anything,' he said.

'Not at all. It's a conversation that's been going on for years.' I glanced at my watch. 'I'd better get going.'

'You're still okay for our drive?'

'Absolutely. Looking forward to it.'

Wishing him goodnight, I headed off down the pavement and to the alley behind the restaurant where I'd parked my car. Once behind the steering wheel, I lay my head in my hands and took a deep breath. I felt exhausted and sick. Maybe I overreacted to George. He'd been trying to mend bridges, and I'd cut him off. Still, it was easier to mend bridges when you were the one who'd destroyed them first. It wasn't so easy being the other party.

I tried starting my car. The engine didn't respond. Trying again, I said words that my mother wouldn't have liked, and the engine still didn't turn over. Groaning, I climbed out. It was a quiet night, although I could hear the distant sound of people in the restaurants along Percy Street.

My gaze moved to the building across the street: Primbee Funeral Directors on William Street was quiet.

Always the quietest place in town, I thought.

I put the hood up and peered at the motor.

'Who am I trying to kid?' I muttered. I knew so little about engines it could have been on fire, and I wouldn't have noticed. 'I need help.'

The pounding of feet on pavement came from behind me as I took out my phone. Then a figure wearing a balaclava emerged from the darkness, crashed into me, and I was sent flying.

26

'Can you describe him?' Todd asked.

He was sitting opposite me at our kitchen table as Nan placed cups of tea and plates of biscuits before us. I took a sip of the tea. It was hot and sweet and just the right thing to ease my shattered nerves.

'It was dark,' I said. My shoulder hurt from where he'd knocked me to the ground. My arm wasn't in great shape either. In stealing my bag, he'd twisted my forearm badly. 'I couldn't make out any details.'

'Why didn't you call the police?'

'I got saved by Wayne from the diner. He heard me yelling, came to my rescue, and the guy ran off. It was all over in seconds.' I held up my phone. 'Thank goodness I had this and my keys in my hand, or I would have had to walk home.'

Wayne had checked the engine, and found the hood had been forced open, and one of the battery cables disengaged. The person who stole my purse may have wanted to create a diversion so they could grab my bag. Wayne had reconnected the battery, and my old jeep had started without a problem. Then I'd rung the bank to cancel my cards, so at least my assailant couldn't go on a spending spree.

'Have one of these, Todd,' Nan said, waving the biscuits before the policeman. 'You're wasting away to nothing.'

Despite my injuries, I had to laugh.

'Thanks, Nan,' he said.

'You're welcome. You know that Rosie's still single—'

'Nan!' I yelled.

'—but she doesn't like me mentioning it for some reason.' Unable to hide her smile, she disappeared into the kitchen. 'I've got some washing up to do.'

'Ignore her,' I sighed. 'She's totally senile.'

'I heard that!' Nan yelled from the kitchen.

Todd smiled, then grew serious. 'Is there any chance you were attacked by Charlotte?'

'No.' I considered it. 'At least, I don't think so. My mugger was taller.'

'Can you remember anything about their clothing?'

'Not really. It was dark. A stupid place to leave my car now that I think about it. The lighting doesn't work in that car park. It's as dodgy as the restaurant.' I shook my head. 'I've cancelled my credit cards and reset a bunch of passwords on my accounts, just in case.'

'That's wise.'

'But I hate losing that bag. Everyone loved it—even Colin Wood.'

'Is there any chance that he could have stolen it?'

I laughed. 'It was an expensive handbag, but I'm sure Colin can afford his own.'

Todd finished his tea, and I showed him outside. The evening was clear and dark as we walked to his police car. Leaves rustled in a nearby tree.

'That's Possy,' I said.

'Ah, your ringtail possum. Watch out. Maybe he mugged you.'

'I doubt it. Possy's got morals.'

Todd got into his car and started it before winding down the window. 'Be careful.'

I promised I would, and he drove off. As he reached the corner, Nan came onto the verandah and leaned on the railing. 'Is that handsome policeman gone already?' she asked sweetly. 'I thought he might stay the night.'

'Nan!'

My grandmother chuckled, and we headed inside.

Later, as I climbed into bed, I thought about the disparate parts of this case. None of it seemed to connect together. My mind returned to something Dorothy had said. She'd seen someone leave the inn with a bag, head to Mermaid Point, and return empty-handed. There was only one explanation: whatever they'd taken had been tossed into the water.

It wasn't the murder weapon; that had remained firmly implanted in Katy's chest. It couldn't have been the real ring. Something that size didn't need to be carried in a bag. And the thief wouldn't have disposed of it by tossing it off a cliff.

I awoke the following morning with a renewed sense of optimism. Today was a big day. The World Record Attempt was being held, and I was interviewing Spud Butler. Plus, there were other things I needed to do. I had a plan. I knew how to move ahead in my investigation, but it wouldn't be easy.

Still lying in bed, I spent the next few minutes finding the contact details for Oscar Farrell. He and his brother Tony owned Cape Carson Scuba, and I'd written a few stories about them and their business over the years.

Ringing Oscar, I explained what I had in mind. He was less than enthusiastic.

'Diving off Mermaid Point?' he said. 'That's a challenging dive.'

'I don't need you to do the dive,' I said. 'You know I've got my diver's certificate.'

I'd gotten my Open Water dive certificate through them.

'I know, Rosie. But what's that saying about fools rushing in?' I could hear him scratching his unshaved face. 'The water at Mermaid Point is rough at the best of times.'

'It's my choice.'

Oscar sighed. 'When were you thinking of going?'

I said as soon as possible. We agreed to meet later at the wharf. That's when the tide was incoming. Thanking Oscar, I hung up and lay back. *What next?* The latest edition of the Gazette would be in everyone's hands this morning. That might bring something.

My phone beeped. Colin.

I've had a call about a job, and need to send them some info. Can we take a raincheck on that scenic tour?

I sent a message back.

No worries.

It was a relief anyway. I had a million things to do. I showered and soon emerged a few minutes later, feeling ready to face the day. Well, almost ready. Fortunately, I'd tossed my old handbag into the wardrobe and brought it back out again. I restocked it with some makeup and an old change purse.

I threw on a dress decorated with a bright flower pattern and headed to the living room, where I found Nan and Dave eating pancakes.

'She's alive!' Nan announced.

'You had doubts?' I asked.

'I was just about to come in and check your pulse.' Nan indicated the stack. 'Sit down and grab some.'

Dave looked sheepish. 'I might have cooked too many.'

'Not if you invited the entire population of Cape Carson for breakfast.' I told them I was heading into town to grab a coffee. 'I'm leaving the car and walking.'

'Walking's good for the mind,' Nan said.

'So true,' I agreed.

Heading out the door with Trixie by my side, we went down the road to where it met bushland. Here, I followed the trail to Cut Rock Lookout, where I stopped to gaze at the ocean and away to the horizon. It was another perfect day, with just a few white clouds bubbling in the distance.

I sent Kim a text telling her I was going to Sandy's for a quick coffee, and she said she'd meet me there. Starting down the path towards the beach, I'd only gone a few feet when Trixie turned and gave a bark.

'Hello!' Todd said. He had his three-legged greyhound, Rocko, at his side and was quickly making his way down the hill. 'You're out early.'

'You know what they say about the early bird.'

'Haven't beaten up any more muggers?'

'Not yet. But the day's still young.'

We headed towards town. My eyes settled on the lighthouse and the platform at the top. I wondered again about Katy and the letter *C*. She had tried to identify her killer. It had to be someone staying at the inn. Charlotte was obviously mentally unstable. She seemed the most likely suspect, except the scheme seemed too involved for her to carry out.

Cameron was a suspect, but he and Cindy were together at the time of Katy's death. Cindy was awake at two-thirty when Cameron had posted images to social media. They could have been in this whole thing together—except Cindy didn't seem that emotionally engaged with Cameron. Their entire relationship seemed precisely as they'd described it: a fling. Plus, the deal on Katy's new film would financially benefit them both. Why kill Katy when their financial boat was about to come in?

Then there was Colin. He didn't have an alibi, but would he go to the lighthouse to kill Katy? Could he have had some deep abiding hatred of her? Not likely. He seemed to have gotten on with his life. They could have argued, and things got out of hand. But that didn't explain the knife.

This was a premeditated murder. Someone went to the lighthouse expressly to kill Katy.

The last person on my list was Chadek. He had no reason to kill her either. The bodyguard knew there was something bogus about the ring. He could have swapped it. But why hint that there was something wrong with the Horizon Ring? And why kill Katy?

This was getting me nowhere. The obvious killer was the person who'd already been arrested: Chris.

'A penny for your thoughts,' Todd said.

I looked at him in surprise. 'Sorry,' I said. 'I was just thinking about the case.'

'Don't you know that all work and no play makes Rosie a dull girl? Are you ready for the world record attempt? That's on this afternoon.'

'I know. Dancing's not my strong point, but it's for a good cause, so I'll do it.' I glanced at him. 'Talking about dancing, will you be wearing your dancing shoes?'

'I'm helping with crowd control.'

I laughed. 'Ah-ha! You're not a dancer!'

'I am! I just don't like to show off!'

Still laughing as we reached the bottom of the hill, I told Todd I was interviewing Spud Butler later.

'This is certainly a week for celebrities,' he said. 'Katy and Cameron Dark...Spud Butler...'

'Rosie Ryan,' I added.

'Yeah, her too.'

Lots of people were out and about on the coastal path. Plenty of visitors who'd come to town for the Festival were taking early strolls. Probably trying to wear off some calories, I guessed. Some familiar joggers appeared on the path ahead of us.

'Hey!' Amanda called out. 'You're out early!'

Her eyes flickered between Todd and me as she and her husband Tom drew to a halt. The men nodded to each other. I told them about my mugging the previous night and my stolen bag. Amanda was furious and wanted to track the thief down. I laughed and said everything was fine. I just had to buy a new bag.

'Your mum's been telling me how much she loves to dance,' Todd said.

'Mum's got the moves. Especially after a few gins.'

'That's not true!' I protested.

'Have you forgotten Uncle Joe's sixtieth birthday party?'

I had—momentarily. 'Let's not go there,' I said. 'And I'm not a dancer. My feet end up going in the wrong direction, and I never know what to do with my arms.'

'It's a tough issue,' Todd agreed, with mock severity. 'What do we do with our arms? Punch the air? Flail like zombies? Or go with the classic karate chop?'

'Huh?'

'You know,' Todd said, delivering a not very groovy dance move while karate chopping the air. 'See?'

'Hmm,' Amanda said.

'Right,' Tom agreed.

Rocko and Trixie whined.

'That's terrible, Todd,' I said.

'Thanks, Rosie,' he replied, unconcerned.

Again, Amanda's eyes flickered between Todd and me, and I knew it was time to get moving. I wished them both well, and they continued on up the hill. I strolled along the coastal path before saying goodbye to Todd and turning off to Sandy's. Kim was already waiting for me, drinking a glass of water at one of the outside tables. She'd obviously already been for a run.

'Is everyone in this town exercising?' I asked.

'Pretty much. Great, isn't it?'

'Should be a law against it.'

Sitting down, I ordered my usual jumbo double-shot caramel latte from a waitress. By the time it arrived, I'd already filled Kim in on my morning and told her about the previous night.

'Mugged?' Kim said. 'Here in Cape Carson?'

'I know. Weird, right?'

'That's twice in the last couple of days. First, that woman Charlotte tried to kill you, and now some random stranger steals your handbag.'

'It's unusual.'

'And these people don't even know you.'

'Yes, imagine what it would be like if they actually knew me!'

My phone rang, and I glanced at the screen. Wanda Gibson? *I wonder what she wants.* Hopefully, it wasn't anything to do with the contest.

'Wanda,' I said. 'How are you on this lovely day?'

'Fine, fine.' Her booming voice came down the line. 'Just wanted to touch base with you. We always do that with the judge to apprise them of the complaints.'

'Complaints? Er...really?'

Wanda barked a laugh. 'Never fear, Rosie,' she said. 'There are *always* complaints. You may have broken the record, however. Thirty-two emails, fourteen phone calls, and a dead chicken in my front yard at four in the morning.'

'A dead chicken?' I said, alarmed. 'That's terrible.'

Wanda chuckled. 'Never fear. It's all part of the fun and games surrounding the Cupcake Festival. There was one year when Harry was judging, I had a live crow stuffed through my letterbox. Took me half an hour to shoosh it out of the house. Sent my cat, Bastet, into a frenzy.'

'Gosh.'

'There was something that piqued my curiosity. A Facebook message arrived asking for your home address. The sender's account was new and obviously bogus. Their profile picture was a British Shorthair. A very attractive cat.' She paused. 'Not enough to make me share your address, however.'

Thanking Wanda, I hung up and related the conversation to Kim.

'That's a worry,' she said. 'Could it be Charlotte?'

'Maybe. The police still haven't tracked her down.'

'She might be stalking you, like in that book, *Peggy Hates*

Veronica. It was set for the Cape Carson Mystery Book Club a few months back.'

'Oh yes. I almost read that book.'

'It's the one where Peggy, the psychopath, plots revenge against Veronica, the journalist, who she says ruined her life. Veronica only survives by pushing Peggy into a paper folding machine. I really liked it.'

Kim liked anything with blood and guts. 'You would.' I sent a text to Nan telling her to keep an eye out and not open the front door to any strangers. Especially women who looked demented. She immediately sent a message back saying she didn't open the door to strangers, demented or not.

I told Kim that I'd arranged with Oscar and Tony Farrell to go scuba diving.

'Into the Cauldron?' Kim said. 'Are you crazy? That place is dangerous.'

'I'll be fine,' I said airily. 'I'll give up if it gets hairy.'

Kim was about to say more when my phone beeped. It was a reminder that I had to get to my meeting with Spud Butler. 'I'll see you later,' I told Kim.

Trixie and I hurried back home, where I jumped in my jeep and cut across town to the Kilkenny Arms, one of the most upmarket hotels in town. Although set two streets back from Percy Street, it still had a good view of the water and a nice bar downstairs.

That was where Spud Butler was waiting. Sipping a coffee with his manager, Laura Gelding, he was reading the latest edition of the Gazette. Spud had won a Golden Guitar award at Tamworth the previous year and had a number one hit song across the country. He had a young John Denver look about him: slightly goofy-looking, clean-shaved with an untidy mop of straw-coloured hair. He climbed to his feet and gave me a firm handshake.

'Welcome to Cape Carson, Spud,' I said.

'Thank you. I've just been reading one of your articles. Must be nice covering a story that doesn't involve murders.'

My eyes angled to the Gazette. 'Murders don't happen that often around here,' I assured him. 'And I prefer good news stories anyway.'

Whereas Spud had a friendly untarnished look, Laura looked like a female shark that someone had stuffed into a suit. Despite being about thirty, her hair was platinum blonde and her face angular and hard.

'Rosie,' she said. 'I hope you realise we're here doing this of our own accord.'

'I know. And the town appreciates it. The local hospital will benefit from all the money raised.'

Spud spoke up. 'We're happy to help,' he said pointedly to Laura. 'Anytime.'

We sat down, and I asked Spud about his career. Most of

what he had to say was information I already had. How his father had named him Spud on a dare. That his mother had gotten him into music. The time he'd spent in the local church choir. His first band which had led him to branch out on his own. Working through my list of questions, I finally got to the question I generally left till last.

'Is there anything else you'd like to add? Anything that springs to mind?'

Spud thought for a moment. 'I've had plenty of ups and downs,' he said. 'A lot of things didn't go right. For a while, all I could see was the bad side of things.'

'So what changed?'

The singer shrugged. 'My perspective,' he said. 'Laura was helpful. She said it all came down to how you looked at life. Sometimes you need to see things from a new angle.'

'Thanks,' I said, nodding. 'That's great advice.'

27

It was a quieter morning in the office. Everyone was always more relaxed the day after we went to print. I put together part of my story about Spud Butler performing the world record attempt. I could write the rest after it was completed. Then I told Jay and Ellie about having my handbag stolen.

'Things do get taken,' Ellie said. 'We've had some farming equipment stolen at Wattle Farm.' She and her boyfriend Ralph lived on a commune with a dozen other people several kilometres north of town. 'Was this your super magical *Russell Fletcher* handbag?'

'It was the love of my life,' I confirmed. 'Well, after my daughter...and my mum...and Nan....'

Jay glanced over from his computer. 'Do we count as loved ones too?'

'Absolutely,' I assured him. 'But that bag, well, it was near the top of the list.'

I spent the rest of the morning working on the Spud Butler

story in addition to a follow-up to my Katy Dark article. My focus this time was on Chris. Although I didn't like doing it, we needed a background story about him. Chris was the main suspect and, unless there was a break in the case, he would go to jail for her murder.

Lunch came and went. Soon it was time for the world record attempt. After saying a quick ta-ta to everyone, I jumped into my jeep with Trixie and drove home to change my shoes and pick up Nan and Dave.

'I wonder how they went with registrations,' Nan said as we climbed into my car.

'I don't know,' I said. 'Everyone's got to be registered so they can be counted for the world record.'

Leaving Trixie at home, I drove into town and parked near the Gazette office. Large numbers had turned out for the event. People were everywhere. Although there were faces I recognised, many I didn't. It looked like most of the southwest corner of Victoria had heard about the attempt. A lot had turned up in fancy dress. I spotted people dressed as cowboys, aliens, and ghosts. There was even a group dressed as dinosaurs.

'Wow,' I said. 'This is bigger than I expected. I didn't know so many people liked line dancing.'

'It's not the line dancing,' Nan said. 'Or even the world record attempt. It's Spud Butler.'

I quickly got quotes from a few people for my article and

snapped several photos. Then we found a spot to stand on Percy Street near the old cinema. Further down, the road had been blocked off, and traffic was being diverted away from the beach. A flatbed truck with loudspeakers on both ends sat across the intersection of Percy and Donovan Streets.

Dave gazed about in amazement. 'Look at this,' he said. 'I've never seen so many people in town before.'

Amanda and Tom spotted us and came over. I peered across the sea of heads, spied Kim, and waved. She pushed through the crowd with Sandy from the diner.

'I thought you'd be at work,' I said to Sandy.

'And miss all the fun?' Sandy said. 'Not a chance!'

A figure strode onto the stage, and I'm sure there was a collective eye-roll from most of the crowd as they recognised Mayor Lynch. The blonde grabbed the microphone.

'Residents of Cape Carson!' she said. 'Welcome to this Guinness Book of Records attempt for the Largest Number of People Dancing Mabel's Cupcake Shuffle.' The crowd cheered. 'Isn't Cape Carson the greatest place in the world?' Again, there was lots of cheering. 'We're privileged today to have a famous guest. He's the winner of last year's Golden Guitar. He's the one...the only...Spud Butler!'

The crowd cheered as Spud and his band strode onto the stage.

'Now,' the mayor continued, 'there's an election coming up

next year—'

'Thank you, Mayor Lynch,' Spud said, taking the microphone from her and saving the day. 'Are we all ready to dance?'

This time the crowd went wild.

Spud waited until the cheering finished before asking everyone to form lines. We all needed room to do the steps. Most people would have seen his video on social media, but Spud took us through the moves anyway. The excitement in the crowd was building with each passing moment.

Amanda came and stood next to me. 'Shame your man friend couldn't be here.'

'Todd?' I said and reddened.

She elbowed me. 'Ah-ha!' she said. 'So Todd *is* your man!'

'He's about as far away from being my man as...as....' Well, I wasn't sure what. 'We have just as many agreements as we do disagreements.'

Nan leaned around Dave. 'Amanda,' she said. 'Are you asking about Rosie's boyfriend?'

'Nan!' I groaned.

'I've told him he can stay over any night. We've always been broadminded in our family.'

'Nan!'

'Our house is double-brick. Dave stays over all the time, and Rosie doesn't hear a thing—'

Kim burst out laughing at my shocked expression, and even

I had to grin. By now, Spud Butler had demonstrated the dance, and he pushed back his hat.

'Are we ready to dance?' he asked.

The resounding roar was so loud they probably heard it in New Zealand. The band played the opening notes of the song, and Spud started singing the verses:

Have you heard about Mabel?
She used to live by me.
A harder working lady,
You'd never ever see.
She'd hustle up some dinner
For all the kids in town.
Then she'd give a yell:
'Come and set yourself down!'
The kid's would see the greens,
And vegies to the roof.
Sayin, 'Mabel, don't you know
Kids have a sweet tooth?'
Hands on her waist,
But giving them a smile,
Mabel would shake her head
And say, laughing all the while...
'Cupcakes can be yours
But eat up what you got,

You're still a growing bunch,
You're gonna grow a lot.
'Eat up all your greens
And your other vegies too.
Then have some cupcakes
And join our dancing crew!'

The town was already dancing. Everyone was doing their own moves. But now we'd reached the chorus, and everyone was ready for the shuffle. Spud Butler took a deep breath and sang:

It's one step to the left
Then one step to the right
Then jump up and turn all around.
Take another to the right
And another to the left
And finish with a shimmy going down!

Although I wasn't sure if it would be enough to take out a world record, there was something I did know: this was a special day in Cape Carson.

Thousands of people were doing Mabel's Cupcake Shuffle. The crowd shimmied, jumped, turned, and bobbed for as far as the eye could see. This had to be one of the biggest days the town had ever known.

The song finally ended, and the crowd let out a huge roar. Spud thanked everyone for their contribution. Mayor Lynch returned to the stage to add her congratulations.

After Spud and his band left the stage, the mayor tried to remind everyone about the upcoming election, but the crowd was already dispersing. Everyone was heading to the beach or finding something to eat. Sandy took this as her cue to get back to the Diner.

'Wait until we get the rock and roll festival going,' she yelled over her shoulder. 'It'll be huge!'

I told Nan and the others that I'd see them later. They all disappeared into the crowd except for Kim, who took me aside.

'We need to talk,' she said. 'It's about this dive.'

'I'll be fine.'

'That's easy to say. What if something horrible happens? The Cauldron is a tricky place.'

'Nothing's going to happen. I'm with experienced divers. If it seems too difficult, I'll get out of there.'

Kim fixed me with her sternest gaze. 'Rosie Ryan,' she said. 'You're a crazy person. It's too dangerous.'

I promised her again that I'd be careful, and she reluctantly wished me good luck. I navigated through the crowds to the wharf where Tony and Oscar Farrell were waiting on their boat, the *Lady Slipper*.

'Right on time!' Oscar Farrell said.

'You're not exhausted from all the dancing?' Tony asked.

'I can dance all night!' I said. 'Or half the night, anyway.'

The two big men grinned broadly. Although they weren't twins, Tony and Oscar Farrell were often mistaken for such.

They were big men with curly brown hair and a perpetual three-day growth. I'd interviewed them a few times over the years about scuba diving and the local sea life.

Tony started the boat. We cast off from the dock and headed around the breakwater into the open ocean. Out here, the water was choppy, and an onshore breeze had picked up. I pointed into the distance.

'That's a lot of cloud,' I said.

'Rain's on the way,' Tony confirmed. 'It'll be here by nightfall.'

Reducing speed, we turned and aimed for the lighthouse. Along the base of the cliff ran a narrow rock platform. Waves crashed uniformly against the stretch of rocks except for the spot where the mermaid lay on her tiny rocky island. Around this, the water churned and seemed to lap in all directions.

'That's the Cauldron,' Tony said, pointing. 'Underwater, the rock platform angles down into a bowl shape. The waves either strike the mermaid's rock or go around both sides to meet in the middle. That's what makes it so rough, even on a calm day.'

Oscar cut the engine twenty metres from the Cauldron and tossed out the anchor. The *Lady Slipper* came to a slow stop. The men went into the change room to get ready for the dive. Technically, I was doing this alone, but Oscar and Tony were prepared to jump in if I got into trouble.

I got changed, emerging several minutes later. Oscar did up the zipper on the back of my wetsuit.

'We thought you'd disappeared in there,' he said, laughing.

'I didn't pull the suit up far enough.' It was a rookie mistake. Putting on a diving suit meant putting your legs in first, then pulling the suit up all the way to your crotch. If you didn't pull it up high enough, it meant the shoulders were impossibly tight. It took me three attempts to get it right. 'I forgot how heavy all this stuff is.'

'It's easier once you're in the water,' Tony said.

He was correct, of course. The suits were made of neoprene, a buoyant material. Without using weights to take you down, you'd float on the surface like a cork. What allowed you to sink or rise in the water was the combination of weights and the BCD—Buoyancy Control Device. The BCD on this suit was a vest that fitted over the torso. Controls on it allowed me to inflate it to rise, float or release air to descend.

We all checked each other's equipment.

Tony and Oscar were far more experienced than me, but

checking their equipment also reminded me of my own. Everything was in place: tank, fins, snorkel, mask, and mouthpiece.

'You're definitely fine with this?' Tony said. 'One of us can go if you want.'

I hesitated. 'Thanks,' I said. 'But I can't ask you guys to do this. Especially seeing as how there's some risk involved.'

'We have dived here before,' Oscar said. 'But it's about the last place we'd come to. Even on a good day, the cauldron is a mess. The water surges in all directions. Sand gets tossed around, so visibility is poor. Stay aware.'

I said I would. The guys got me to run through the diving basics: clearing my mask and eustachian tubes and the importance of descending and ascending slowly. Going down or up too quickly could cause the bends.

Oscar lowered the transom platform at the back of the boat.

This would allow me to take a giant stride entry into the water. Plodding onto the platform, I held my breath—and then forced myself to breathe normally. Holding your breath while diving was a no-no. I inserted the regulator into my mouth and took a few normal breaths. Giving the guys a final nod, I stepped off the boat and into the water.

There was a splash and then an explosion of water and air bubbles. After clearing my mask and popping my ears, I slowly swam for the Cauldron. The guys were right. The water was a mess. My previous dives had been in calm, clear water. Here, water surged in all directions, and it was messy with strands of seaweed and moving currents of sand. Releasing air from my BCS, I slowly descended until I reached a depth of about twenty metres. It wasn't as rough down here, but the visibility was even worse.

Oh dear, I thought. *This won't be easy.*

I slowly swam into the Cauldron's 'bowl' and made a slow loop of the edge. In the centre sat the pillar of rock upon which the mermaid rested. Beneath me, the bottom was an uneven surface of stone, seaweed, and sand. Halfway around, I spotted something poking from the bottom. Swimming closer, my curiosity was dampened after a moment as I realised it was a handlebar.

Someone's dumped their old bike into the ocean! I thought. *Idiot!*

I continued on.

After completing a loop of the Cauldron, I crisscrossed the bottom. The next half an hour passed quickly as I methodically searched the area for whatever had been thrown into the water.

If I'd been searching for treasure, I would have been sorely disappointed. The sea bottom produced a shopping trolley, soft drink cans, a bottle, and—incomprehensibly—a vacuum cleaner. Nothing seemed a likely object that a killer would discard after a murder.

The one bright spot was some of the sea life: a few schools of tigerfish, some weedy sea dragons, and a crab that went scurrying away under rocks. Despite the surging water, it was still peaceful down here.

A shape moved through the water to my left. At first, I thought it was a large fish. As it drew nearer, however, I realised it was a fur seal. The creature paused momentarily and then, deciding I wasn't a predator, made a slow loop around me. It continued around the cauldron, exited back out into the open water, and disappeared into the murky distance.

I checked the gauge on my tank. My air was getting low. If I didn't find something soon—

My eyes focused on a piece of seaweed swirling about in the water. I'd spotted it before and not given it a second glance. Now I saw it wasn't seaweed. It was a piece of rope. Swimming over, I saw it was attached to a bag almost the same colour as the sand.

This is it.

The bag was tied tightly. I gave it an experimental tug. *Heavy.* Although I had no idea what was inside, the bag and the rope were new. Whatever it was had only been recently deposited. The bag and its contents were too heavy to tow back to the surface. It meant I had to use a different manner of getting it onto the boat. Slowly dragging it across the ocean bottom, I reached the anchor point where the *Lady Slipper* lay moored. After attaching the rope to the anchor, I gradually ascended to the surface, where I was greeted by Tony and Oscar's welcoming faces. My arms were jelly after the dive. The guys helped me into the boat, and I pushed back my mask.

'You made it!' Tony said, relieved.

'You didn't think I would?'

'We were taking bets,' Oscar said. 'Especially after seeing that shark.'

'What?'

Oscar chortled. 'Kidding.'

While they helped unhitch my tank and remove my gear, I told them about attaching my treasure to the anchor. They asked me about the weight of the bag.

'I'm not sure,' I said. 'Maybe three or four kilos.'

'That shouldn't be a problem,' Tony said. 'Any idea what's in it?'

'None.'

Untying the bag, I peered inside, not sure what I'd see.

What is this?

Turning the object over, my mouth fell open as I finally understood what had been thrown into the ocean.

Oscar hovered over me. 'What is it?'

'Something strange,' I said. 'Although this is finally starting to make sense.'

28

'Thanks for coming,' I said. 'I'm so pleased you could make it.'

'We were hardly given a choice,' Cameron complained. 'We were practically ordered here.'

'I'm sorry about that, but I thought it was important to have everyone here.'

I gazed around the assemblage of people sitting around the dining room of the Lighthouse Inn. There was a strange déjà vu about the scene. The staff members—Sheila, Dorothy, and Jason all sat around a coffee table to one side. Guests from the night that Katy was murdered—Cameron, Colin, Cindy, and Chadek—were all seated at the dining table.

Katy wasn't there, of course. She was dead. Neither was Charlotte. Her whereabouts was still unknown, although Todd had told me that sightings of her had come in ranging from Cape Carson to Sydney.

Kim and Todd were here too. Kim sat nearby while Todd stood near the doorway. If there were a violent uproar in the next few minutes, I knew Todd could deal with it. If he couldn't, half a dozen police officers waited outside who could.

At the vacant end of the dining room table sat a box.

Although no one had commented on it, everyone's eyes had flickered to it more than once.

Well, I thought. *You'll all know soon enough what's inside.*

'The sooner this is done,' Colin said, 'the better.'

'I agree,' Cindy echoed, glancing at Chadek. 'Though I must say I'm surprised to see *him* here.'

The bodyguard shrugged. 'What is it you Australians say? I'm a surprising kind of guy.'

I turned to Todd. 'We're still missing someone.'

The policeman nodded and called, *Send him in*. Everyone in the room stared expectantly at the door. There was a collective gasp, however, when it opened.

'Chris!' Kim said.

Cameron leaped to his feet. 'This is outrageous!' he said. 'That man should be in jail!'

'No,' I said. 'He shouldn't. Chris Dawson is completely innocent.'

'What? What do you mean?'

'Rosie?' Colin broke in. 'What's going on? Why are we here?'

'This is insane!' Dorothy said. 'I'm not sitting in the same room as a killer!'

Only Chadek looked calm. 'I don't know what is happening,' he said, a smile playing on his lips. 'But I think we should stay to watch.'

'Please do,' I said to everyone. 'It took a lot of work for me to understand what happened the night of Katy's death. And now I know who killed her and how they did it.'

This revelation was met with deafening silence.

'Okay, Rosie,' Todd said, finally. 'Tell us.'

I took a deep breath and began. 'There were two crimes,' I said. 'The first was the murder of Katy Dark, and the second was the theft of the Horizon Ring. I'll begin with the lesser crime first, the theft of the ring.

'The biggest mystery regarding its theft was how it was done. The ring was locked in a safe. It should have been—no pun intended—safe, and yet it wasn't. Somehow, it ended up under Chris's pillow.' I paused. 'I think we can all agree that someone smart enough to break into a locked safe would also be smart enough to find a place to store the stolen goods. Instead, the ring was left in the most childish place imaginable: under a pillow.'

'So you're saying it was planted?' Jason said.

'Oh yes,' I said. 'And I never would have ever worked out how it was done if not for Dorothy. She spotted someone leave the inn after two-thirty in the morning. The person, carrying a bag, was headed for Mermaid Point. When they returned, the bag was gone.

'Mermaid Point is a dangerous place. The water below the cliff face is known as the Cauldron. At least three people have drowned there over the years. Whoever dumped that bag into the Cauldron wanted it gone. But what could it be?' My eyes scanned the assembled faces. 'I had to find out. And the only way to do that was to scuba dive into the Cauldron.'

'It's not an easy place to dive, but fortunately, I had two experienced divers with me. It took a lot of searching, but I finally found the bag. I got it back to the boat and opened it up. I had no idea what it would contain.' I went to the cardboard box, opened it, and lifted out the object. 'I certainly didn't expect *this*.'

Everyone stared.

It was finally Chris who spoke. 'Is that...is that...'

'It's a safe,' I said. 'A *replica* safe. It's designed to fit over the real safe in Katy's room. From the outside, it looks just like the normal safe. It opens from above and it's a little larger. The interior is shallower to accommodate the real safe, but otherwise, it's identical.'

Sheila spoke up. 'No.' The woman looked close to tears. 'We run an honest place here. I would never—'

I nodded. 'I know, Sheila. You're just another innocent pawn in this whole story. This theft took a lot of preparation.

Months of it.' I pointed to the false safe. 'Normally, the hirer of the room can set their own combination. There's a master combination for each safe, but that's held by the company in Zurich. This safe is different. The thief stayed at the inn a few months back. They asked for the View Room, knowing it was the room that Katy would use. They measured the real safe to work out what had to be built.

'You can imagine Katy arriving the other day. She was told there was a safe in her room, and so she deposits the ring inside. She suspects nothing. Why would she?' I paused. 'Except this safe isn't like the others. We checked with the safe company. This one opened when Katy entered her code, but it also stored her code so it could be read by the thief.

'The next morning, when we discovered that Katy had been murdered, all hell broke loose. The police turned up. They were everywhere. The thief panicked. They had to hide the real ring in a place that would never be searched. But where was that? It had to be somewhere where no one would think to look.'

Colin cleared his throat. 'You don't mean under Chris's pillow?' he said. 'Because that was an obvious hiding place.'

'No,' I said. 'It wasn't hidden under Chris's pillow. Colin, you put it in the most unlikely spot of all. You put it in my handbag.'

29

For a long moment, the only sound was that of the distant surf.

Colin forced a laugh. 'You're making a joke,' he said. 'You must be—'

'You stole the ring the night Katy died. You did it when everyone was still downstairs at dinner. You were the first one to leave. Using your own code, you went into Katy's room and swapped the rings. It would have only taken a minute. I encountered you in the hallway. At the time, I thought you may have been hanging around waiting for me, but it wasn't that at all.

'Of course, your work was only half-done. You still had to remove the replica safe. Knowing that Katy often went to her lover's room in the middle of the night, you were awake and waiting for her to leave. When she didn't go to Chris's room but instead left the building, it made no difference. If anything, it was easier for you.

'You entered her room and used a small crowbar to remove the replica safe. Although it must have come as a surprise when you saw the fake ring was gone, you realised Katy had obviously taken it with her. You set the real safe code using Katy's code which had been stored by your false safe. When she returned, Katy would enter the code and deposit the fake ring.

'Next, you went to Mermaid Point and tossed the replica safe over the edge. A mistake you made was to not throw the crowbar in as well. I suspect, in the heat of the moment, you only remembered it as you returned to the inn. You then tried to hide it in the barbeque out the back.'

Colin's face had gone beetroot red. 'Rosie,' he said. 'This is silly. Just a story—'

I barged on. 'You made two mistakes, though. The first was dropping the replica safe.' I gave the false safe a shove. 'This thing has quite a bit of weight to it. Both Charlotte and Chris heard a thud around half-past two. That was you dropping the safe on the floor of Katy's room. The second error was being seen by Dorothy. She saw the thief leave for Mermaid Point and return empty-handed. However, other than those mistakes, you would have gotten away with the perfect crime.

'The next morning, Katy would never notice that the safe looked slightly smaller than before. Weeks, months, or years could pass without Katy and Cameron revaluing the ring.

Eventually, it would be revealed as a fake, but no one would ever be able to determine when the real ring was stolen.'

I paused. 'Except Katy didn't return to the inn,' I said. 'Early the next day, all hell broke loose when the news spread of Katy's death. You panicked. Stealing a valuable ring was one thing, but murder was something entirely different. Especially the death of Katy Dark.

'You had to put the ring somewhere that the police wouldn't find, but also where you had a chance of retrieving it later. My new *Russell Fletcher* handbag must have seemed ideal. The bag had dozens of pockets. Even I hadn't opened them all. And what better place to hide a ring? Todd and the other officers know me. They know I'm not a jewel thief or murderer.' I shot Todd a small smile. 'Any examination of my belongings would be cursory. It was much more likely that the criminal was someone else. A stranger.'

I stared directly at Colin. 'Of course, once you hid the ring, you had to get it back. At Sandy's Diner, you probably hoped I'd leave my bag at the table, but I didn't. Later, you assaulted me in the car park and stole my bag.'

'It's...no...you're mistaken....'

'I didn't bother investigating the loss of my handbag. Not until I realised it was where you hid the ring. That's why I asked Primbee Funeral Directors on William Street to check their video footage. Fortunately, their camera covers that entire section of the street. And, of course, there you are with my bag.'

Colin tried to speak. He had gone very pale, and his eyes had filled with tears. 'I didn't...I mean...' he said. 'But I needed the money! I could sell it...retire...'

'You murdered my wife!' Cameron Dark snapped, leaping to his feet. 'And after everything Katy did for you! You killed her!'

'Sit down,' Todd ordered.

'But he killed my wife!'

I spoke up. 'Colin didn't kill your wife.'

'What?' Cameron looked stunned. 'Then who did?'

'Sit down, and I'll tell you.'

Reluctantly, the actor retook his seat.

'As I said, there were two crimes that night,' I said. 'The first was Katy Dark's murder. The other was the theft of the Horizon Ring. I've told you how the second crime was done. Now I'll let you know how the first happened.

'To begin, we all know the evidence that pointed to Chris. He was having an affair with Katy. It was his phone that was used to lure her to the lighthouse. The same message told her to bring the ring. It seemed to be a straightforward case of robbery and murder.

'But for a moment, let's look at everyone else who was at the inn that night. After dinner, Dorothy confronted Cameron before returning to her room for the night. They both lied to us, but we discovered the truth.'

Dorothy spoke up, a note of defiance in her voice. 'It's no big deal,' she said. 'Not really. Cameron Dark is my father. We spoke about it the other night.' Her eyes settled coldly on him. 'It's fair to say that we're still working through our issues.'

'I'm not the fathering type,' Cameron said, not looking at his daughter.

I continued. 'Who else is there? Sheila?' I inclined my head to her. 'This dear woman had less motive than anyone. What about Jason? He left early as he always did and had no access to that part of the building where the key was located. Besides, none of these people could know about the secret phone.

'So let's look at the other guests. We know that Colin was awake. We know because he was about to steal the ring. Everyone else was asleep: Charlotte, Chris, Chadek, Cameron, and Cindy. The question is: who stole Chris's phone and lured Katy to the warehouse? Could Charlotte have killed Katy? Not likely. She couldn't have known about the phone or the affair. And Chadek? He had no motive to kill Katy. However, he suspected later that the ring was fake.' I turned to him, as did everyone else in the room. 'The police took you up to the room the next morning. My guess is that you looked at the safe and realised it looked different. Not a lot different. Most people wouldn't have noticed it, but I bet you did. The second you saw it, you understood how the robbery happened. Your history is a little shady, so you thought it best to say nothing.'

'Is that true?' Cameron snapped.

Chadek folded his arms. 'I make no comment,' he said. 'I know nothing about these things.'

I'm sure you don't, I thought dourly.

'And then there's Cindy and Cameron: the couple with the unbreakable alibi. Cindy had no reason to want Katy dead. Killing Katy would be like cutting off her arm. Now, who does that leave? Cameron. Did he have a reason to kill Katy? Here the answer is yes. Not because Katy was having an affair. But because of one of the most fundamental reasons of all: revenge. Cameron had a successful career before he met Katy. He was the star of Horseshoe Farm. After meeting Katy, he was no longer the star but a bit player. His career was over.'

Cameron Dark's mouth had dropped open. Now he spoke up. 'Rosie,' he said. 'You almost make it sound as if it were me who killed Katy.'

'You did, Cameron,' I said softly. 'You murdered Katy Dark.'

The actor stared in astonishment, blinked, and let out a bitter laugh. 'You...*idiot!*' he said. 'You *stupid* woman! How dare you accuse me of murdering my wife. You know I was with Cindy when my wife was murdered! You said so yourself: we have an unbreakable alibi!'

I ignored him. 'Here's how it happened,' I said, turning to the others. 'It seemed they were both together, but they weren't. By the time midnight came, Cameron had already stolen the burner phone from Chris's room. He then sent a message from it to Katy at twelve-twenty-five, asking to meet her at the lighthouse at two-thirty. At twelve-thirty, he went to Cindy's room. Although Cameron says he stayed there for the rest of the night, that's only partly true. Knowing that Cindy regularly took sleeping pills, he secretly gave her one, and she dropped off to sleep. After some time, he got up, turned the clock forward an hour, woke her up, and told her it was *two-thirty*. She blearily woke up and asked what he was doing, and he said he was posting photos to social media.'

I turned to him. 'But you weren't. You were just pretending. Cindy wouldn't have noticed. She was groggy. The important thing was that she had to look at that clock and verify the time. You'd hidden Cindy's phone under the bed in case she later woke up and tried to find it. Of course, you wanted other people to sleep soundly too. You didn't want them waking up during the night on the off chance they spotted you. Despite this, I awoke that night. I was tired and didn't spot that something was wrong. Something missing. It was only yesterday that it struck home.'

Todd frowned. 'And what was that?'

'The grandfather clock didn't chime.' I let this settle in. 'I was up and about at that time, and there was no gong. It's because Cameron disabled it. He didn't want it waking people up during the night. Cameron, you went to the lighthouse, killed Katy and stole the fake ring. You then posted photos to social media.

'When you returned, you restarted the grandfather clock, reset the clock in Cindy's room to the correct time, and climbed into bed.' I paused, thinking of what it must have been like for Katy, turning up at the lighthouse to meet Chris. She must have gone through the open door and climbed the steps in anticipation, expecting to find Chris waiting for her at the top. Her excitement must have turned to confusion and then horror when Cameron appeared—brandishing a knife.

'After murdering Katy,' I said, 'you needed to do one last thing. You had to pin the crime on Chris. The next morning, when everyone started running about madly, you returned the burner phone to Chris's room and planted the ring under his pillow. You didn't know the ring was a phony. How could you?'

I turned to the others. 'And if the charges didn't stick against Chris, there were always the threatening letters. I suspect at least one of them was from Cameron. The one supposedly found on Katy's pillow was almost definitely written by him. Katy's death could be blamed on a random stalker. As it turned out, we had one here anyway: Charlotte.'

Cameron Dark's face was twitching. 'This is so...*ridiculous*,' he stammered. 'A fantasy. You've made it all up in your head, you stupid woman. You have absolutely no evidence—'

'We have two pieces of evidence,' I said. 'Todd fingerprinted the interior of the grandfather clock earlier. Your fingerprints were found.'

The actor paled. 'How did you know—'

Todd hesitated. 'We don't formally have your fingerprints on file,' he said. 'But we were able to lift them from your room for comparison. There's no reason your prints would be *inside* the clock.'

Cameron Dark's mouth trembled, but he remained silent.

Kim spoke up. 'Rosie, you mentioned the second piece of evidence?'

'That came from Katy,' I said. 'The mysterious *C* that she wrote with her own blood.' I shook my head. 'It never made sense. Why would a dying person write that letter knowing it was so ambiguous? It could only have meaning if it pointed to something other than a person's name. Then I remembered something that Spud Butler told me.'

'Which was?' Chris asked.

'He said his life changed when he altered his perspective. He said it all depended on how you looked at things. And he was right. We looked at what Katy had written and thought it was the letter *C*.'

Kim frowned. 'And it wasn't?'

'No. From where we stood, it looked like a *C*. From where Katy lay dying, it wasn't a *C*; it was a *horseshoe*. It pointed right at Cameron, who was the star of Horseshoe Farm.'

Cameron Dark fell back in his seat, his resolve broken. 'You can't understand what it's like to be famous,' he said. 'One day, I was in the spotlight. People would stop and point and say *There he is! Cameron Dark! He's a star!* But then I left the show and I became anonymous. I became *nothing*. I'm not sorry I killed her. Now all the headlines will be about me!'

'Yes, Cameron,' I said sadly. 'I suppose they will.'

30

'Ah-ha!' I said as I stumbled sleepily into the kitchen. 'It's finally done.'

Nan was perched over the kitchen table, wearing a pleased expression. The three thousand-piece jigsaw puzzle of the city of Rome had been almost completed the previous night. Nan must have gotten up early to do her morning yoga routine and put in the final pieces. Pushing back my messy hair, I peered down at the image.

'Wow,' I said. 'Those Romans knew how to live.' The panoramic view of the city showed a metropolis impressive by anyone's standards. 'Rome was huge.'

'And you know these things take time.'

I rolled my eyes. 'Nan. Don't say it.'

'Say what? I was just going to say—'

'Don't!'

'Rome wasn't built in a day!'

Groaning, I headed off to shower and get ready for the day.

Soon, I was on my way down to Sandy's with Trixie at my side. A storm had come through during the night, and more showers were expected. The sky was a jagged mess of graphite clouds and the ocean a mass of white tips. Only a few people walked along the coastal path, huddling inside jackets as a stiff onshore breeze pressed against their backs.

'It's a cold one,' I said to Trixie. She barked. Hot or cold, I didn't think she minded much. Just so long as we were out walking. Reaching the diner, I left her under the awning and grabbed one of the window seats. I was only there for a minute when a figure came racing along the footpath. I waved, and Kim came bounding inside.

'Hey, you!' Kim said. 'Eating anything?'

'Only coffee for now.'

We ordered and were soon sitting back in quiet bliss. The Cape Carson Cupcake Festival was done for another year. The contest was completed, a world record had been set, and—most important of all—Katy's case had been solved.

Kim leaned forward. 'Guess what?'

'What?'

'Chris and I went out last night.'

'I see. How was it? Has the old love been rekindled?'

'Well, we kissed.'

I gave an approving nod. 'Wow,' I said. 'Fast work. So it's on again?'

Kim bit her lip. 'Not exactly,' she said, sitting back. 'Actually, it's a bit like Grease Two. Some sequels should never be made.' She stared out at the water. 'That summer was a special time, but I'm a different person now. So is Chris. While he's not a bad guy, he's not my type. We were talking and…he doesn't like reading.'

'*What?* How can he be a writer if he doesn't like reading?'

'Beats me. Anyway, when Chris said the last book he read was years ago, I knew it would never work. He's already left town. I said goodbye to him last night.'

I sighed. 'The perfect man isn't easy to find.'

At that moment, I spotted two familiar figures on the other side of the road. George and his brother Nico were out for an early morning walk. Nico looked as rough as ever, and I wondered if he ever showered. At least George was presentable. I sipped my coffee.

'So what's happening with George?' Kim asked.

'Nothing. And it's not going to.' I told her he and Blossom weren't getting on. 'I think it's time we all moved on.'

'I'm sure the right men are out there for us. We've just got to find them.'

Kim finished her coffee, glanced at her watch and said she had to head off to work. Just as she reached the footpath, Kim frantically waved to someone further down the road. I followed her gaze. Todd. Kim pointed to the diner.

That Kim, I thought. *She never gives up!*

Todd had been taking Rocko out for a walk. Leaving him with Trixie, Todd came in and was soon nestled into the seat beside me. He ordered his espresso, and we watched the view as rain splashed against the window.

'You did an amazing job with that case,' Todd said.

'Thanks.'

'You could have saved me some time, though.' He looked at me with mock severity. 'I dropped into the funeral directors on William Street yesterday.'

I tried to look innocent. 'Really?'

'Yes, Rosie. Turns out Primbee Funeral Directors doesn't have security cameras.'

'Oh, right.' I reddened. 'Yes, I was bluffing, but I had to get Colin to confess. At least you picked up on the fingerprints inside the clock.'

'Would have been nice if you'd given me some warning you were going to lie about that. That means you were bluffing twice. Remind me never to play poker against you.'

I smiled. 'I was betting that Cameron wouldn't have worn gloves while he turned the chime lever on the clock.'

'And if he had?'

'Then I would have tried something else.'

Todd peered out at the rain splattering against the window. 'I've been thinking.'

'Yes?'

'Well. Three things. First, it would be handy for me to have someone to chat to about cases.' He stared at me. 'Did your eyebrows just shoot up?'

'Yes! I've been saying for ages we need to work together!'

'I'm not talking about working together. All I'm saying is that it would be handy to discuss cases with you occasionally.' He glanced around to make sure no one else could hear. 'But it would have to be off the record.'

'I promise. And what else did you want to mention?'

'We were talking about dinner. Somewhere nice. Not that horrible Super Thai place you mentioned.'

I burst out laughing. 'It is pretty awful,' I admitted. 'I bumped into Mayor Lynch yesterday, and she said they were looking at closing it down. Anyway, let me think about it, and we can work out somewhere nice.' Now that I thought about it, there was also our planned walk along the beach. 'And what else?'

'The ring! It's still missing! You know we interviewed Colin, and he said it wasn't in your bag. That means someone else took it. It's missing.'

'Do you think it could be one of the other guests? Could it be Charlotte?'

'No. The police picked her up in Warrnambool yesterday. The poor woman is quite unwell. She'll be institutionalised for some time.'

I nodded. Both Cameron and Colin were in jail. Chadek, Cindy, and Chris had all left town. The person who'd shot Chadek had been identified as a member of a Melbourne crime gang, and had been arrested. The unofficial band known as the Six Cees had broken up, and the chances of the band ever getting back together were zero.

I reached into my bag to take out my purse and pay. 'It's all very strange,' I agreed. 'I wonder what happened to the ring.'

'That's what I've been wondering—*where did that come from?*'

Todd's eyes were wide with amazement.

'This old thing?' I said, waving my hand about. 'It's a bit gaudy, but it's got something about it.' I removed the Horizon Ring from my finger and took one last regretful look at it before handing it over to Todd. 'It's that awful Super Thai restaurant. When I was out with George, I dropped my bag and everything—including the ring—fell out. Remembering that Super Thai was never properly cleaned, I wondered if the ring could still be there. I went there yesterday, looked under one of the tables, and there it was, tucked in behind a table leg.'

Todd turned the ring over in his hand. 'This is amazing.'

'Yeah.' I stared thoughtfully at the ring. 'But it's only a ring. It's not as good as the really important things in life: friendship, family or...love.'

Todd's eyes angled up to meet mine. A silent understanding passed between us. I wondered if anything would ever eventuate between us. Our careers seemed to be a wall between us. Maybe his offer to discuss cases with me was a step forward in breaking that wall down.

By now, the rain had stopped, and the sun was trying to come out. Bright shards of light were spotlighting the ocean. We paid up and went outside to unleash our dogs.

'A quick stroll around the lighthouse?' Todd asked.

I looked towards the iconic building and remembered that last photo I'd taken of Katy. She had seemed so peaceful as she stood on the gallery enjoying the view. The lighthouse was a magnificent place, full of history, both good and bad. The death of Katy Dark was part of that history now. Still, the future lay ahead, and I was sure that Katy would have wanted people to enjoy their time in the sun.

'Sure.' The sky grew brighter. 'Why not? It's a beautiful day.'

But the adventure doesn't end here!

Catch Rosie's next mystery in:

Knives, Knots and Murder!

ABOUT THE AUTHOR

Darrell Pitt is a prolific author, with more than two dozen novels in print. Writing for both young and old alike, Darrell's books traverse multiple genres including cozy mysteries, science-fiction and adventure stories. A proud resident of Melbourne, Australia, Darrell shares his home with his wife and says he owns too many books (as if such a thing were possible!)

His literary journey began with a passion for crafting short stories in his youth, eventually evolving into full-length novels. Among his accolades, "A Toaster on Mars" earned a prestigious spot on the shortlist for the 2017 Russell Prize, showcasing Darrell's unique brand of humour. His novel, "The Firebird Mystery", received commendation from The Children's Book Council of Australia as a Notable book in 2015.

Darrell's Teen Superhero series has garnered widespread acclaim, while his Rosie Ryan books are a series of delightful mysteries set in a distinctly Australian environment. Among the books he's currently working on are a tech-thriller, a time-travel novel, and a mystery book set in 1960's Victoria.

9 781923 360402